LADY GUNSMITH

1

The Legend of Roxy Doyle

Books by J.R. Roberts
(Robert J. Randisi)

Lady Gunsmith series

Coming Soon!
The Three Graves of Roxy Doyle
Book 2

The Gunsmith series
Books 1 -150

Angel Eyes series
The Miracle of Revenge
Death's Angel
Wolf Pass
Chinatown Justice
Logan's Army

Tracker series
The Winning Hand
Lincoln County
The Blue Cut Job
Chinatown Chance
The Oklahoma Score

Mountain Jack Pike series
Mountain Jack Pike
Rocky Mountain Kill
Comanche Come-On
Crow Bait
Green River Hunt

Visit: www.SpeakingVolumes.us

LADY GUNSMITH

1

The Legend of Roxy Doyle

J. R. Roberts

SPEAKING VOLUMES, LLC
NAPLES, FLORIDA
2017

The Legend of Roxy Doyle

ISBN 978-1-62815-669-0

PROLOGUE

Along the Mormon Trail
1866

Eleven year old Roxy Louise Doyle stood in front of her father, his hands on her shoulders, as the Wagonmaster—in lieu of a proper man of God—read from the scriptures over her mother's grave.

Roxy had still not recovered from the Indian attack of the day before. Up to then the trip from Philadelphia had been a pleasant one for her. Unburdened from the stress the adults had to endure, all she had to do was enjoy the sights as the landscape passed by, first on a train, then a stagecoach and, finally, when they reached and joined the wagon train that would ultimately take them to California.

But they had barely crossed the river from Council Bluffs, Iowa into Nebraska when the adults suddenly became concerned about the Indians.

Her father started to keep his rifle with him at all times. Mother kept Roxy close to her. However, when no attacks occurred, the people on the train began to relax their vigilance.

The wagon train was traveling the Mormon Trail, which would ultimately take them to Salt Lake City, Utah where Brigham Young and his Latter Day Saints had settled. Roxy didn't know much about this, except that her mother was Mormon, and her father was not.

The trip was tense, but uneventful, until they reached Wyoming.

When the first attack came, Roxy's mother cradled her, protected her with her own body as arrows rained down upon the wagon train. They stopped and fired back at the attacking Sioux warriors, and appeared to succeed in driving them away.

But a second attack came moments later, with more intensity than the first. It was Roxy's first encounter with blood, as several men around her and Mother were felled by arrows and killed instantly. But again, the members of the wagon train seemed to succeed in driving the warriors away with their rifles.

"Are you all right?" Papa asked his wife and daughter.

"We're fine," Mother said, "aren't we, sweetie?"

"Yes," the frightened child replied. She wanted to be brave for her parents.

An expected third attack did not occur, but as they were readying the wagons to resume their progress Roxy felt her mother's arms tighten around her as a single arrow cut through the air and dug itself into Mother's back.

"I love you, sweetie," Mother whispered in her ear. "Never forget that."

Unaware that Mother was dying Roxy said, "I love you, too, Mother."

It was only after Papa came and unwrapped Roxy from Mother's final embrace that Roxy knew what had happened. She fought to stay with Mother, but they took her away.

The Wagonmaster forced them to bundle her body into the back of their wagon so they could move on before the warriors returned.

That was yesterday, and today they had stopped to not only bury Mother, but the rest of their dead.

Roxy felt cold and numb, unable to accept what had happened. Papa held her, but it didn't help. She cried uncontrollably.

"I'm sorry, folks," the Wagonmaster announced, "but we have to keep movin'. There's no telling when those Sioux will reappear.

"Come along, Roxy," her father said, turning her away from her mother's grave.

As they walked away Roxy asked, "Will we come back and get Mother?"

"No, Roxy," he said, "Mother's body will rest here as she goes on to meet her Maker."

"Us that Mister Young?" she asked.

"No, honey," he said, "that'd be a proper God."

***

As the wagon train continued its progress toward Salt Lake City, Roxy saw her father in deep conversations with the Wagonmaster, and with some of the other families. She couldn't hear what they were talking about, but she knew her father wasn't happy. She thought it was for the same reason she was not happy, because he missed her mother, but it seemed to be more than that.

A week after Mother was killed, Papa pulled her aside to talk to privately.

"Honey, I have to go," he said.

"Go where?"

"Away," he said. "I can't go to Salt Lake City with you and the others. That was your Mother's dream. I'm not Mormon like she was."

"But I'm going with you, right?"

"No, Roxy, just me. You have to stay. You have to finish your Mama's trip."

"But I don't wanna," she whined. "I wanna go with you."

"I know, sweetie," he said, "but I have to find work and make some money for us. I'll be sending it to you so you can have a good life. And I'll come back and visit you from time to time."

He didn't want to have to tell her the truth, his little girl reminded him too much of the wife he had lost. Every time he looked into her green eyes it was like being stabbed in the heart. He couldn't take it.

"But Papa—"

"You'll be stayin' with the Angelo's," her father went on. "They're a good Mormon family, they have two kids of their own that you can grow up with, like a brother and a sister."

"I don't want a brother and sister," she groused, "I want you, Papa."

"Now honey," he said, "you have to be a good girl, for me and for your Mother."

"Mother's dead!" Roxy snapped. "She don't care no more."

"Don't you say that," he scolded her. "Mother's love for you will live forever. Do you understand me?"

"Yes, Papa."

"Now come on," he said. "I have to take you over to their wagon."

"What about our wagon, Papa?"

"I'll be takin' that with me, and along the way I'll be sellin' our things."

"But Papa," she said, "how are you gonna make money?"

She remembered his hand closing tightly over the barrel of his rifle. Years later she realized what it meant, that he was going to make money with his gun. But on that day he said, "I'll be doin' good, honest work."

He walked her over to the wagon, where Mr. and Mrs. Angelo were waiting with their son and daughter. Roxy remembered that this was one of the families she had seen her father deep in conversation with. Apparently, he spoke to several families about taking his daughter, and had chosen Ben and Mary Angelo.

However, Roxy disliked and distrusted Ben Angelo on the spot, and years later she would realize it was with good reason.

PART ONE

Chapter One

Lady G.'s present . . .

Roxy Doyle rode into Kingman, Arizona at the end of a long trail ride. It was a 50-50 proposition who was more tired, her or her roan. To be fair, probably the horse. All she was interested in was getting the horse into a livery, rubbed down and fed, and then getting herself into a hotel, pretty much rubbed down and fed, as well.

There was grit in her eyes and long red hair, which only a bath was going to fix. And there was Mohave dust on her pistol and rifle, both of which had to be thoroughly cleaned.

Kingman was a mining town, made up of ramshackle huts and shacks, and hastily constructed tents. Someone, however, had erected a two story hotel at the South end of town. She knew the majority of the population in a mining town usually lived in tents erected on or near their claims. The hotel catered to the transients, like pickpockets, free-lance whores and drummers.

And Roxy Doyle.

Roxy was too young to have ever been to Deadwood during its hey-day—when Wild Bill Hickok was shot and killed—but she imagined this was what it must have looked and felt like.

She reined in her horse in front of the hotel and dismounted. She was dressed like a man, in a cotton shirt and jeans that accentuated her full figure, boots and holster of weathered leather. Her flat-brimmed Stetson sat atop her red hair, worn at the moment in braids on either side of her head. Trail dust or not, Roxy's beauty shone through, and men turned to watch as she entered the hotel lobby. But she was used to this. She'd blossomed at a young age, and had to deal with the attention of men from that time on. She hadn't been comfortable with it in the beginning, but over the years had learned to use it to her benefit. Now in her mid-twenties, she was comfortable with who she was and how she looked, barely noticing when people stared.

She could tell from the wood and the lobby furnishings that the hotel was very new. The wood even smelled freshly cut. She approached the front desk, and when the young clerk looked up from whatever he was doing, the bored expression on his face changed to one of awe.

"Um . . ." he said, his adam's apple bobbing.

"Do you have a room?" she asked.

Even dry and covered with dust from the desert her face was lovely, and the young man had to wet his lips several times before he said, "Uh, yuh."

"Good," she said. "I'll take one, preferably with no access to the window,"

"Yuh," he said, and reversed the register book so she could sign in.

She signed her name and turned it back, accepting the key he held out to her.

"Do you have bathtubs?"

Apparently, the prospect of her taking a bath was almost more than the young man could take. He blinked and swallowed several times before he said, "Y-yes, Ma'am, in the back."

"I have to take care of my horse," she said. "Can you have a hot bath waiting when I get back?"

"Um, yeah . . ." If he didn't faint, first.

"Where's the nearest livery?"

"A-across the street, just around the corner. It's the last building in town at this end."

"Thanks. I'll be right back for that bath."

"Um . . ." he said, his eyes tearing up a bit.

He watched her walk back across the lobby and out the door, unable to take his eyes from her denim clad, undulating backside, then took out a handkerchief and wiped his face. Only then did he look in the book for her name.

"Roxy . . . Doyle?" he breathed.

The clerk had come from the East for adventure and was well versed in many of the legends of the old west. Kingman had a marshal and a deputy. The clerk knew he had to rush to the lawman's office right away and inform him of who had just registered at the hotel.

Lady Gunsmith was in Kingman.

***

Roxy found the livery, owned and operated by a crusty old timer who seemed immune to her beauty, which suited her fine.

9

"How long?" he asked.

"Maybe a few days," she said. "He needs rest."

"He'll be the only one gettin' any in this town," the man groused. "Ain't nobody rests here." He scowled at her. "You got business in Kingman?"

"I've got business with a bathtub and a steak."

The man's next statement proved that he was not completely oblivious to Roxy's beauty.

"You watch out for the men around here, girl," he said. "Filly who looks like you . . . better be able to use that gun on your hip, is all I'm sayin'."

"Don't worry, old timer," she said. "I can use it."

He stared at her for a few moments, then said, "Yeah, I reckon you can."

She took her rifle and saddlebags off the horse, and allowed the old hostler to walk her animal away.

"She's a pretty little filly," he said, before taking her. "She got a name?"

"No," Roxy said.

"Why not? Horse needs a name."

"Papa always told me never to name something I might someday have to eat."

She left the hostler shaking his head.

Chapter Two

Roxy was relaxing in the hot bath, her gun hanging on a chair right next to the tub, when the door opened.

She saw the man, then the badge.

"Excuse me, Sheriff," she said, "this tub is taken."

"Are you Roxy Doyle?" the man asked. He was tall, broad shouldered, in his forties. The badge was not overly shiny, and had a dent in it. He took his job seriously, didn't sit around his office polishing his badge.

"That's right."

"I heard you were in town," the lawman said. "I'm just here doin' my job."

"And not trying to get a quick look, right?"

"I'm a professional Miss Doyle," the sheriff said.

"What's your name?"

"Gifford, Del Gifford. I've been sheriff here for about five years."

"Well," she said, "I've never been here before, or even near here, so I never heard of you. Sorry."

She gave the man credit. He'd look at her, then look away, not wanting to be caught staring. She maintained a position low in the tub, so that all her good parts were hidden from view, just in case. She wasn't shy, just playing it safe. She didn't know if he was the kind of man she could trust. Not yet, anyway.

"So what's on your mind?" she asked. "I'd like to finish this bath while the water still has some heat."

"I'm just checkin' with you to see how long you plan to be in town," he said. "And what you plan to do while you're here."

"Well," she said, rubbing the soap on the washcloth, which only brought her hands and arms into view, "I don't know how long I'll be in town, but don't worry, I'm not here to do anything but take a bath, get a meal, and sleep in a bed."

"You're not . . . lookin' for someone?"

"Like who?"

"I dunno," he said. "Listen, you have a reputation—"

"Not one I went looking for, by the way."

"But one you have," he said. "Even if you're not lookin' for anyone, somebody might come here lookin' for you."

"That would be their hard luck, Sheriff."

"We're just not used to havin' anybody like Lady Gunsmith in town—"

"That ain't the way I signed the register," she said, cutting him off again. "As far as I'm concerned, I'm just Roxy Doyle."

"Well," he said, "to other people you're Lady Gunsmith. There ain't much you can do about that."

She remained silent, still rubbing soap on the washcloth.

"I just want to warn you," he said. "I wouldn't take it kindly if you killed somebody while you're here."

"I ain't lookin' to kill anybody, Sheriff," she said. "I'm never lookin' to kill anybody, but you best let it be known in town that I won't be trifled with. The men here should give

12

me a wide berth. Pass that word around and things should go fine."

"I'll do that, Miss Doyle," he said. "And, uh, I'm sorry to interrupt your bath."

"That's okay," she said. "As long as you leave now, I can still get some enjoyment out of it."

"Um, yeah, okay," he said, turning to the door. "Normally I'd ask a stranger to turn in their gun while they're in town."

"Not gonna happen, I'm afraid."

"That's what I thought you'd say," he said, "which is why I didn't ask."

"Have a good day, Sheriff."

"Yeah, uh . . ." he opened the door and left, without taking a last look.

Maybe she should have showed him just one leg, to shake him up.

***

She dried off, left her long, red hair loose so it would dry, got dressed and strapped on her gun. Carefully, she opened the door and stepped into the hall. If the sheriff had heard she was in town, so others could have.

She walked down the hall, through the curtain to the lobby, looked at the desk clerk, who seemed nervous. She decided to make him even more nervous.

"So you told the sheriff about me," she said, approaching the desk.

"Uh, Ma'am, sorry, but that's my job," he said. "I mean, part of my job, to let the sheriff know when somebody . . . well, like you, checks in."

"Like me?"

"Um, you know, like . . . famous?"

"I'm not famous."

"Well known, then," he said. "I mean, you have a reputation."

"Who else have you told?"

"No one! I swear!"

"Let's keep it that way, all right?"

"Yes, Ma'am."

"If I hear you told anyone else," she said, leaning in close, "I won't take it too kindly. Understand?"

The clerk leaned back, glassy-eyed, and said, "I understand, Ma'am."

She straightened and said, "Good. Now maybe you can help me."

"How can I do that, Ma'am?"

"Where can I get a good steak in town?"

Chapter Three

The desk clerk directed Roxy to a tent at the end of A Street. As she entered, she saw a woman standing at a stove in the rear of the place, while the rest of it was filled with tables and chairs, about half of which were occupied.

A handsome young man wearing an apron came up to her and stared.

"A table?" she asked.

"Oh!" he said, coming out of his trancelike state. "Yeah, sure. Follow me."

He showed her to a table and she said, "Something in the back, please."

"Uh, yeah, okay."

The people he was going to seat her next to—a man and woman with two young children—looked up at her, the man and woman frowning.

"No offense," she said to them. "I like to sit alone, when I can."

The man and woman looked away, as did the boy, but the girl—about six—smiled at her. Roxy smiled back and waved at her before following the young man to a table in the back, very near the stove where a middle-aged woman was doing the cooking.

"Is she any good?" Roxy asked the waiter.

"That's my Ma," he said. "She's a great cook."

"Good," she said. "I just came off the trail and I need a good steak dinner."

Eager to please the beautiful stranger who just walked in and affected the speed of his heartbeat the waiter said, "I'll have her make you a nice big, thick one."

"Sounds good."

"With spuds and onions?"

"Even better."

"Carrots."

"I don't like carrots," she said. "Double the spuds."

He smiled broadly. "I'll take care of it."

"What do you have to drink?"

"Sorry, just water and coffee."

"Bring me one of each, then."

"Right away."

He ran over to his mother, talked very quickly while pointing out Roxy. His mother looked at her, then nodded to him. He came waking back carrying a glass of water and a cup of coffee.

"Ma's on it," he said. "Can I get you anythin' else?"

"Looks busy in here," she said. "Maybe we can talk later, when you have more time." She flashed him a smile.

The young man, who appeared to be several years younger than she was, nodded eagerly and said, grinning, "Oh yeah."

"What's your name?"

"Dexter."

"Okay, Dexter, we can talk, but after I eat."

"Of course," he said. "I'll check with Ma."

The young waiter ran over to his mother again and said something. She snapped at him and pointed to the stove, where she had more than one steak going. Roxy drank her coffee and waited.

Dexter had other tables to handle, but he kept going back to the stove to bother his mother about Roxy's meal. Finally, she slipped a thick steak onto a plate already covered with potatoes and onions, added a couple of biscuits, and handed it to Dexter. She said something to him shortly, and from the look on her face, it wasn't good.

Dexter rushed to Roxy's table and set the plate down in front of her.

"There you go!" he said, happily.

"It looks great," she said, "but I'm gonna need some more coffee, please, Dexter."

"Dex," he said. "You can call me Dex."

"Okay, Dex," she said, "you can call me Roxy."

"I'll be right back, Roxy!"

He grabbed her cup, ignoring other diners who were trying to get his attention, ran over to the stove and refilled her cup from a large coffee pot, then hurried back with it.

"Thank you, Dex," she said, chewing on her first bite. The steak was perfectly cooked, very tender. Dex was right about his mother. She was a great cook. "Now I just need some time to eat. You better see to your other diners."

"Oh, right," he said. "Ma's kinda pissed with me, anyway, so . . ."

"I get it, handsome," she said. "See you later."

He blushed, which she found sweet, and then went to take care of the other diners.

Left alone, Roxy ate, and enjoyed.

***

She polished off her meal while watching the other diners come, eat and go. All the while, Dex's mother kept tossing her dirty looks. Maybe she thought Roxy was after her young son for some evil purpose.

Poor Dex, she thought. A Mama's boy, through and through.

She washed down her meal with the last of the coffee and water, then waved at Dex, who ran right over.

"What do I owe you?"

"A dollar."

"You sure?"

"I meant that's kinda steep."

"Sorry," he said, "it's Kingman prices."

"Yeah," she said, handing him a dollar. "You know where I can get a beer?"

"There's a saloon tent two blocks down," he said.

"Name?"

"Just says Number Two over the flap," he said. "I could meet you there later, if you want."

She grinned and said, "How would your Mama feel about that, Dexter?"

She walked out before he could answer her.

Chapter Four

Roxy found the saloon tent with a big Number Two over the flap. To get to it she had to pass two others: Number Five and Number Seven. She didn't know why Dex had steered her to Number Two, but he'd been right about his mother's cooking, so maybe he was right about Number Two's beer.

She entered and stopped just inside to have a look. It was afternoon, and the place was teaming with people. Maybe Dex was right about the beer, but she knew that among this crowd were not only miners and businessmen but pickpockets and thieves. There were also pretty girls in flashy dresses working the floor, delivering drinks and ducking grasping hands.

The bar was very long, looked to be made of several old wooden doors laid end to end, supported on wooden barrels. Roxy knew she attracted the male eye whenever she entered a saloon, and this place was no different. She felt them on her as she walked to the bar.

"Excuse me," she said, as men made a place for her.

"Buy you a drink, honey?" one miner asked her.

"I can buy my own, but thanks, sweetie."

One of the men whose eye she had attracted was the bartender. He was a rangy man of about thirty, with dark black hair on his head, his forearms, and sticking out from the neck of his shirt.

"What can I get ya?" he asked.

"Somebody in town told me you had the best beer."

"Coldest, anyway."

"I'll have one."

He went and got the beer, brought it back and set it down, then didn't move away.

"Just get to town?" he asked.

She sipped the beer. "A bath and a steak ago."

"Then first beer's on the house," he said. "My name's Jake, if you need anythin' else."

"Thanks, Jake," she said. "I'm Roxy."

Somebody at the other end of the bar started yelling for Jake, so he rushed down to tend to the customer. She watched him go, interested in the way he moved. She'd been on the trail a long while, some company would not have been objectionable. Maybe that was why she'd flirted with the young waiter, making him blush.

Roxy liked sex and men. She liked them in all sizes, shapes and colors. But life hadn't started out that way. She had problems with the male animal until she learned, at an early age, how to handle them. But she didn't want to think about that, right now.

She turned with her beer, putting her back to the bar, and looked around. Seated and standing, men were drinking and laughing. At some of the tables they were playing poker. Mining and poker didn't mix. So many miners worked all day to dig up a few chunks of gold or silver, then hit the poker table that night to lose it. What was the point? Roxy solved the problem by never mining or playing poker. Besides, she was too damn busy for either one.

The man she was looking for was said to have a penchant for good, cold beer. So if he was in Kingman he'd be in this saloon, sooner or later. All she had was a description, but it was a good one, and for now she didn't see anyone who fit it.

"Lookin' for anybody in particular?"

She turned her head, saw the man on her right, grinning. He was big with grey stubble and yellow teeth, dressed like a miner.

"If you're lookin' fer a man," he said, "I fit the bill."

"If I was lookin for a bear you'd fit the bill," she said. "I'll let you know when that happens. Otherwise I'm fine."

"You got spirit," he said.

"I've got patience, too," she said, "but I'd advise you not to try it. Go back to your friends."

She hadn't seen him with anyone, but men like that usually traveled in packs. To prove she was right, he slunk back to a table full of men, all of whom laughed and slapped him on the back. They all appeared to be miners, and looked like men she'd have no interest in, ever.

"You can handle yourself," the bartender said from behind her.

She turned to look at him. He had blue eyes, which certainly worked in his favor, even if he was a little too hairy for her taste. Still, he seemed fairly clean, and was in good shape.

"I'm used to it by now," she said. She didn't bother telling him that men had started to look at her differently when she turned thirteen, and it hadn't changed since. All that had changed was her ability to handle it.

"Stayin' in town long?" he asked.

"Not long," she said. "I've no interest in mining."

"Or miners, I'll bet."

"You got that right."

"Well," he said, "lemme know if you want another beer, or if you develop an interest in bartenders."

He grinned at her and set off to serve somebody else who was yelling.

She turned back to the noisy crowd and continued to watch while she nursed her beer. Some left, most staggered out, others came in, looking for their first drink, none of them matching the description she had.

At one point she waved at Jake, who must have been watching her, for he appeared immediately.

"Another?" he asked.

"Yep." She put a coin on the bar. "If you don't mind, I'll pay this time."

"Suits me," he said, setting a fresh one down.

She picked it up, "The other saloons in town do as well as this one?"

"They do okay," he said, "but sooner or later everyone ends up in the Number Two."

That suited her.

If and when the man she was looking for walked into the Number Two Saloon, she'd be ready.

Chapter Five

Salt Lake City, Utah
1870

When Roxy was fifteen she learned a valuable life lesson.

By the time she turned thirteen, Roxy had developed in such a way that not only made the boys looking at her, but the men as well. And there were the women of the community. They didn't like the way their men ogled the girl, so they showered her with dirty looks whenever she went outside.

By fifteen she had been living with the Angelo family for four years. During that time she and Grace Angelo had become close. Grace was only a year younger, but was physically changing at a much slower rate.

Danny Angelo was two years older than Roxy, and they never got along. He didn't like his parent's agreement with Roxy's father to give her a place to stay, no matter how much money they received over the years. But that didn't stop him from grabbing at her.

And it didn't stop his father.

It may have been a Mormon community, complete with stringent rules and morning and evening prayers, but Roxy's budding sexuality was still a source of constant attention.

The man she had come to think of as her foster father, Ben Angelo, began not only to look at her differently, but touch her, as well. When she'd walk by him he'd simply reach out and lay a hand on her hip, her butt, or brush against her breasts. He took every opportunity to pull her into his lap, where she encountered something hard and uncomfortable. Roxy made an effort not to get too close to him anymore, and wondered if her foster mother, Mary, even noticed.

Her foster brother was more obvious in his treatment of her. Oh, not in front of their mother, but if they were alone he'd put his hands on her, leer at her, and make comments. Luckily, he was completely inexperienced with girls and didn't much know what to do past that.

Not so the father.

Mary Angelo had put on weight over the years, and while she and her husband still shared a bed it didn't go much beyond sleeping. Very often Ben Angelo would come home late at night, smelling of whiskey and another woman's perfume, so it was no secret what he was doing. This certainly didn't seem like proper Mormon behavior to Roxy.

Her father came to see her once or twice each year, but he didn't want to listen to her complain. Then, suddenly, he didn't appear during the first half of her fifteenth year.

But her fifteenth year turned out to be a seminal one for her. It happened on a day that Mary left the house to go quilting with a group of the women, and Danny went to help with a barn raising. That left Roxy alone with Ben Angelo.

Ben left the house that morning to do some work on their farm, but he instructed Roxy to prepare lunch for him. He came home while she was in the act, moving about the kitchen. He washed up and then sat at the table, watching her.

"You're very good in the kitchen, Roxy," he said. "You move around like a real woman."

She didn't know what to say to the comment. It made her even more uncomfortable than usual around him. When she came to the table with his lunch, he waited for her to set the plate down before reaching out for her.

She flinched, tried to pull away, but abruptly he wrapped his arm firmly around her waist.

"You even feel like a real woman," he said. "Hell, what am I sayin'? You're fifteen now, so you are a real woman."

Holding her tightly with one arm, he used the other hand to feel her thigh, run it up her back to her neck, and then around front to cup one full, young breast.

"Let me go!" she snapped.

"Oh yeah," he said, and she could smell corn liquor on his breath. "You're a woman, all right." He squeezed her breast so hard she cried out. Then he felt for her nipples and pinched one between his fingers.

"Good God, that feels good!" he said. "That's a big nipple, girl. I wanna see it."

And that's when she knew what was going to happen, and there was nothing she could do about it.

Or was there?

He got up from the table, maintaining his hold on her, and dragged her into the bedroom he shared with his wife. Once there he pushed her down on the bed.

"Wait, wait, wait . . ." she kept saying, but there was no waiting. He found her underwear, grasped it and tore it off her.

"Oh please . . ." she begged, but he misinterpreted her tone.

"Yeah, you want it, don't you?" he asked. "Yer a little slut, aren't ya? Walkin' around here ever since you turned thirteen, twitching the butt of yours, stickin' out those teats . . . yeah, you wan' it!"

She realized then that he was the one who wanted it, and he wanted it bad.

"Stop, stop for a minute," she said to him, but kept the fear out of her voice. Then she stopped begging. "Stop!"

"Ain't no stoppin' girl," he said, even though he removed his hand from her crotch.

"You want to see me, right?" she asked. "My breasts?"

"Yer damn right I do."

"Well," she said, "I'll show you. Don't tear my clothes, I'll show you. Stand back."

He was breathing hard, but he did as she ordered. "Yeah, okay, show me."

She slowly drew her blouse down from her shoulders while he watched, licking his lips. And when she stopped just short of revealing anything he said, "Come on, girl, please, don't make me wait." That was the day she realized what she had, and how men would want it. They would beg for it.

She didn't understand the why, only that she was suddenly in control. She couldn't get out of the room because he was in front of the door, blocking it, but she thought she could keep him from being too violent with her, keep him from hurting her too much.

He moved in on her once she was naked to the waist . . . it felt odd to her, and frightening, but also—and she hated to admit it—kind of good.

When he was done, he went back to the kitchen to eat his lunch. She cleaned herself up, got dressed, and never told her foster mother what happened when she came home . . .

***

Thereafter, when he had sex with her, it was more on her terms than his. When they were alone he'd approach her, but often she made him beg before giving in, and while she still considered it rape, she also learned from the experience. Learned what to do to a man that would give her more and more control.

And then it happened with Danny . . .

***

Her foster brother was seventeen at the time. Roxy was working in the barn, feeding the stock, when she heard the barn door close behind her. She turned and saw Danny standing there, looking odd. Then she realized he had the same hungry look on his face that his father had, and she knew what was going to happen.

But it was going to happen her way.

"What do you want, Danny?" she asked.

"You know what I want, girl," he said. "I want what you been givin' Pa. I saw the two of you last week. I want it, too."

"You do, huh?" she asked. She took off the gloves she'd been using to feed the stock and tossed them aside. "You want this?" she asked, touching her breasts, "and this?" she touched her crotch.

Danny looked feverish. "Yes! I wan' it!"

"Come here, then."

He approached her, and she put her hand out to keep him at arm's length.

"Beg for it," she said.

"I ain't gonna beg."

"Why not?" she asked. "Your Papa begs. He begs me to touch him, to let him touch me. You want what he gets, don't you?"

"Yes, damn it!"

"Come on, then," she said, her hands going to his belt, "let's get these off of you."

She undid his trousers, dropped them to his ankles, then did the same with his underwear.

"Oh, God," he breathed.

"You like this, huh?" she asked.

"Oh yeah . . ."

"Beg me," she said.

"Aw Roxy . . ."

There was a pitchfork nearby. She realized, years later, she could have picked up the pitchfork, threatened him or even stabbed him, but at that moment she felt powerful—and there was another thing she had to admit to herself. She enjoyed sex, as long as it was on her terms.

"Beg!"

"Please," he said, "pleasepleaseplease . . ."

She grinned at him, the stupid boy whose eyes were just about rolling up into his head . . .

***

The next day the rest of the family went out, Mary Angelo convincing her husband and son to visit a neighbor with her, leaving Roxy home with Grace.

"What are you doin'?" Grace asked, coming into the room while Roxy was packing.

"I'm leaving, Grace."

"But . . . why? Where are you goin'?"

"Just away," she said. "I can't stay here anymore."

"What will you do?"

"I'm gonna look for my father," she said.

"But Papa says we ain't heard from your Daddy in so long he must be dead."

"He's not!" Roxy said, turning so abruptly that Grace flinched. "He ain't dead, and I'm gonna find him."

"But . . . why can't you stay here?" Grace asked.

Roxy wanted to tell Grace why, but she couldn't tell the girl what she had been doing with her father, what she'd done with her brother just the night before. And at the same time, she was worried about the younger girl, but those two wouldn't do the same thing to their own kin. But Grace was still a little girl, even at thirteen, gangly and flat-chested. Roxy hoped the girl would stay that way.

She wrapped up her belongings as best she could in a blanket, and lifted it.

"I love you, Gracie," she said, giving the girl a one armed hug.

"I love you too, Roxy," Grace said. "Will we ever see each other again?"

"We'll see each other," Roxy said. "I promise."

She went out the door, left the farm, and never went back.

Ten years later she was still looking for her father . . .

Chapter Six

Kingman, Arizona

Roxy's present . . .

Gavin Doyle had become a bounty hunter.

And a legend.

It had taken Roxy a couple of years to find out about her father, the reputation he'd built doing what he did to send money to the Angelo family. Since then, she hunted for him, or people who knew him, investigated rumored sightings, even though many people thought he was dead.

What had brought her to Kingman was the tip that a man named Harlow knew where her father was or, at least, what had happened to him. Armed with just a last name and a description, she nursed her second beer and watched, waited. The only other thing she knew about Harlow was that he made his way with his gun, so she was going to have to be careful. She didn't want to have to shoot him before they talked.

She had been in the Number Two for a few hours when the flap opened and young Dexter entered. He looked around, spotted her at the bar and smiled.

During that time she had rebuffed half a dozen men, four had simply slunk away, but two had become angry, and spent the past hour or so drinking heavily. She was expecting trouble, and was hoping that Harlow would walk in before it happened. What she didn't need was a lovesick young waiter getting in the way.

"I was hopin' you'd be waitin' here," he said.

"I am waiting," she said, "but not for you."

"But I thought—"

"Go home, Dex," she said. "This place is too rough for a nice boy like you."

"You're a girl and you're here."

"I'm a woman," she said, "you're a boy."

"Roxy—" He reached for her and she pulled her arm away.

"You got trouble?" the bartender asked, from behind her.

"I'm fine," she said. "He was just leaving."

"Will I see you again?" Dex asked.

"Maybe," she said. "Now go. The person I'm waiting for is not a good man."

He pointed his finger at her and said, "This ain't over."

Sweet, stupid boy, she thought, as he went back out through the flap.

She turned to see the bartender still standing there.

"Lovesick boy?" he asked.

"You could tell?"

"I'll bet you've left a lot of those behind."

"One or two," she said. "Not my fault."

"Probably not. Another?" He looked at the empty mug in her hand.

"One more's my limit," she said.

He went and drew the beer, brought it back and handed it to her.

"Whoever you're waitin' for," he said, "he's a fool for keepin' you waitin'."

"Thanks."

"Who would that be, anyway?"

"Just a man," she said.

"Not your man?"

"No."

"Too bad for him."

She raised the mug to him and said, "Thanks." She dug out a coin and dropped it on the bar. He picked it up and went to tend to other customers.

She turned, saw two men standing in front of her. They were the two who had reacted angrily when she rejected them.

"Bitch," one of them said.

"You like to tease men, don't ya?" the other asked.

They both wore trail clothes and guns, not miners, just passing through. They had approached her separately but had used her rejection to band them together.

"You two should go and sleep it off," she told them. "You're drunk."

"Not too drunk to take care of you," one of them said.

The other reached out for her, and she swatted his hand away.

"I won't let you lay your hands on me," she said.

The first man gave her an ugly grin and said, "Relax, you're gonna like it."

"I'm warning you."

They laughed, and both reached for her.

She tossed the rest of her beer into the face of one, drew her gun and shot the other one square in the chest. She could have simply cold-cocked him with the weapon, but she had been taught never to draw her gun unless she was going to use it. So as soon as it cleared leather, there was only one possible result.

The second man wiped beer from his face with one hand and, with an angry growl, reached for his gun. She shot him, also in the chest. It only took a few seconds, but they were both dead. If she'd shot them in the belly they would have lived a while and bled out. The chest was more humane, killing them instantly.

It got quiet.

She ejected the two empty shells from her gun, and everyone heard them hit the ground. Reloading, she returned the weapon to her holster, turned to find Jake looking at her from behind the bar.

"It was their call," he said, loudly.

Everyone was still frozen, watching,

"Somebody get these bodies out of here," Jake called out.

Immediately, four men stepped forward and dragged the corpses out to the street.

"You got another beer comin'," Jake said to her, and set it on the bar.

"Thanks."

People started moving again, and talking, and in seconds she was being ignored. There were no other men in the place who wanted to suffer the same fate.

"The law will be here soon," Jake said, "but everybody saw it. Those two didn't give you a choice."

"I warned them."

"Yeah, you did."

"No man touches me unless I want him to."

"I'll keep that in mind," he said. "Just stay here and drink your beer. When the law shows up, you'll have witnesses."

"Thanks, Jake."

"Sure, Roxy."

Chapter Seven

Jake the bartender was right on the money.

Fifteen minutes after the bodies had been dragged out, Sheriff Gifford entered. He looked around, spotted her at the bar and walked over.

"I thought we had a good talk," he said.

"We did," she said, "while you were peeking."

"I was not—" he stopped himself short. "You killed two men, Miss Doyle. They're lyin' out in the street."

"Do you want to charge me with shooting them, or littering?" she asked. "Because I had nothing to do with putting them out in the street."

"That was me, Sheriff," Jake said, from behind her.

"Jake," Gifford said, "stay out of this."

"Can't do that, Del," Jake said. "I'm a witness. Those two men pushed her, and she had no choice. Then I had them dragged out of my place. Dead men can be a health hazard."

"Maybe your place is a health hazard, Jake."

"No Del," Jake said, "you've had enough drinks in here to know that's not true.

Roxy looked at the sheriff and raised one eyebrow.

"Never mind that!" Gifford said. "We had a deal, Miss Doyle!"

"Ask around, Del," Jake said. "There are plenty of witnesses. Those two forced the action. I'm tellin' you, she had no choice."

Several men standing nearby nodded their heads, agreeing with Jake.

"I can see you've got the men in here on your side," Gifford said to her.

"I've got nothing to do with that, except for being in the right."

Gifford rubbed his hand over his face. "Looks like I've got no choice but to believe you."

"That's because it's the truth," Roxy said.

Gifford frowned, then looked past her at the bartender. "Jake, stop tossin' dead men out into the street."

"I'll do my best, Sheriff."

Several men laughed, and the sheriff stormed out.

Roxy turned to the bar. "Thanks, Jake."

"Del's an okay guy, Roxy," Jake said. "He's just tryin' to do his job."

She nodded and looked around the place.

"Seems like the commotion might have scared your guy away," Jake said.

"Looks like," she said. "I'll have to try again tomorrow night."

"Want another one for the road?" he asked.

"No," she said, "thanks. I ain't hitting the road, just going to my hotel." She looked him in the eye and said, "Room Seven."

He nodded as she turned and walked out.

Chapter Eight

It was no surprise when the knock came at her door. Jake the bartender did not strike her as a stupid man.

"Sorry it's so late," he said, as she opened the door.

She reached out, grabbed him by the front of his shirt, and pulled him into the room. Pausing only to slam the door she then turned and pushed him down on her bed.

"See, I don't close," he said, as she undid his belt, "so I had to get somebody to handle the bar."

She pulled off his boots, then yanked down his trousers and drawers. For a hairy man he didn't have much of a bush, but there was a very nice cock standing out from it, already getting hard. It was long and smooth, not veiny at all, which suited her. The pretty dick made up for the mass of hair on his chest.

She had already removed her gunbelt and her own boots, so it took no time to shuck her shirt and jeans. She stood there naked for a moment, giving him a good look at her pale skin, her large, heavy breasts, large rust-colored nipples and copper pubic bush.

"Damn!" he said.

That was all the time she gave him. She'd been on the trail a long time, and she needed this. So she got up on him, straddled him, reached between them to grab his cock and guide it to her already moist pussy. She rubbed herself on him, wetting him with her juices, then allowed the head of his dick to poke at her before finally settling down and letting him slide inside.

She leaned forward, put both hands flat on his hairy, muscular chest and started riding him up and down, slowly at first, and then increasing her speed as she sought out her own pleasure with very little thought of his.

He didn't seem to be complaining, though. He grunted and groaned as he tried to move his hips in unison with hers, coming up off the mattress to meet her, at the same time stroking and grabbing her breasts with his hands and his mouth as they gently bumped against his face.

Roxy felt the sweat start to slide down her back and face, also between her breasts. Still she sought her orgasm, eyes closed, brow furrowed, grunting with the effort until finally she felt it build . . . and build . . . and build . . . and then she was almost bouncing on him, her muscles seeming to have a mind of their own . . .

***

Later, as they lay on their backs, side-by-side, she ran her hand down over his belly and into his crotch, taking hold of his penis and stroking it. To her delight, it began to get hard, again.

"Ah, not done yet, are you?" she asked.

"Not with a woman like you," he said.

"Well, let's see."

She slid down until she was lying on her belly between his outstretched legs. Continuing to stroke his cock until it was rigid, she then brought her mouth down on him, taking him inside, wetting him thoroughly before starting to suck.

Jake's eyes rolled up and he let out a long, guttural groan as he gave himself up to the actions of her mouth and hands. She gripped his cock at the base with one hand, massaged his balls with the other while continuing to work him with her lips and tongue. Before long he was bellowing as his prick ejaculated into her mouth. She took every drop and then kept sucking for more until it was almost painful for him . . . utterly beautiful, fantastic pain.

"Jesus . . ." he said, when she released him. "What a woman you are."

"You liked that, huh?" she asked, coming up to lie beside him again.

"I sure did."

"And you want more?"

"Oh, yeah."

"Well," she said, "maybe another time, if you're real nice, and maybe you beg a little."

"Beg?" he asked.

"But now I have to get some sleep," she said, "so it's time for you to go."

"Why can't I stay the night?"

"I don't think so," she said. "I need my sleep. I was on the trail a long time."

"Well," he said, sitting up, "when can I come back?"

"I don't know, Jake," she said, eyes closed, "we'll have to see." She turned her back to him, curled up, knowing that he wouldn't be able to stop staring at her ass. "Good-night. Make sure you pull the door shut on your way out."

Nothing happened for a few seconds, then she felt him get out of bed, heard him dress. Pulling the door closed behind him, perhaps a little too hard, he was gone.

And then he was forgotten and she was asleep.

Chapter Nine

When she woke the next morning, the sheets still smelled of Jake and their lovemaking. She was going to have to ask the desk clerk to make sure they were changed. Jake had scratched an itch for her, but that was it. She was done with him, except in his position as a bartender.

She didn't know what she was going to do with her day. Harlow probably wouldn't be hitting the saloons until that night, unless the shootings of the night before frightened him away. But from what she knew about him, she doubted that was the case. He hadn't been described to her as a man who was afraid of much.

Kingman was more mining camp than town. Finding ways to entertain herself would be difficult. Meals, beer, maybe sex with somebody other than Jake. Or maybe just finding a place to sit and watch the street, in case Harlow rode in, or walked by.

She got dressed, strapped on her gun and went down to the hotel lobby. The clerk watched her warily as she approached the desk.

"I need fresh sheets," she said. "I'd like them to be there when I get back."

"When will you be back, Ma'am?" he asked.

"I don't know," she said, turned and left the hotel.

It had rained overnight, so the streets were muddy. A buckboard had broken a wheel right in front of the hotel, and two men were trying to lift it so they could repair it. Women skirted the puddles as best they could, while men splashed through them without a thought. That's what men were like, single-minded to the point of being messy, slovenly, dirty. She could count the men she'd met and respected on the fingers of one hand, and still have digits left over to hold her gun.

She walked down the street, drawing looks from men and women alike. She had left her red hair free flowing, falling to her shoulders from beneath her flat-brimmed hat. She knew some men were looking at her because of what had happened in the saloon the night before. And there was a difference in the looks she got, when they were born of lust, or of respect, or fear. Or even curiosity. From women, she got looks of jealousy as well as curiosity. She knew some women resented her because of her beauty, but also because of who she was; a free woman making her own way in the world without depending on a man.

And she knew it was a man's world. Who would be silly enough to think otherwise? She also knew she had already made her mark, and would continue to do so.

And she remembered very well when she'd made it the first time . . .

***

Abilene Kansas, 1875

Roxy was twenty years old.

She'd left Salt Lake City five years ago, had been making her own way since then, and it hadn't been easy. A girl on her own, in her teens, who looked the way she did, had to fight off a lot of boys and men who thought she was an easy target. It was only a couple of years after she lit out that she started to carry a gun, stuck into the front of her belt. It was a Navy Colt she had come across in her travels. Way too big for her, but at the time she felt she needed a big gun to make her point. When she pointed it at a man, holding it in two hands, they left her alone.

She had not been raped since the incidents with her foster father, but had come close several times. Guile had helped her more than once, other times it was her feminine wiles, but most times her beauty gave her the upper hand. Men were both crude and cruel, and did most of their thinking, at least around her, with their dicks. Soon she had learned to use their weakness against them.

When she rode into Abilene on a small pony she had managed to buy several months earlier, she drew looks from people on the street. She wore no hat, and had her long red hair in a ponytail. She refused to cut it. She liked it long, and it was a useful tool—that, and the way she filled out her cheap chambray shirt and jeans. More than once she had been offered jobs as a saloon girl, or a whore, and turned them down. One Madam told her that with her looks she could make a fortune as a whore, but five years out of Salt Lake City she was still bound and determined to find her father, or learn what happened to him.

For the past few months Roxy had been trying a new strategy. Instead of talking to shopkeepers and bartenders, she would hit a town and start with the local law. So she rode directly to the sheriff's office, dismounted and tossed her horse's reins over a hitching post.

She looked around, then mounted the boardwalk and read the shingle next to the door. Marshal IRA DOKES. She entered the office.

Abilene's days as a rough Cowtown were behind it, at that point. The position of Marshal was best known for the terms of Bear River Tom Smith and Wild Bill Hickok. But the town didn't need men like that, anymore, so the badge fell to men of lower stature and reputation.

The marshal of Abilene at this time was a large, red-faced man in his fifties. He looked from his desk as she walked in, then dropped the wanted posters he'd been going through onto the desk top. He looked her up and down, pausing not on her hair or breasts like most men did, but on the Navy Colt in her belt.

"What can I do for you, girlie?" he asked.

"Have you ever heard of Gavin Doyle?"

"The bounty hunter?" he asked, sitting back in his chair. His gunbelt and hat were hanging on a hook on the wall. He had a halo of grey hair around a bald head, and a belly that flowed over his belt. "Ain't he dead?"

That wasn't what Roxy wanted to hear.

"I mean," the marshal said, "I heard he was dead. What's it to you?"

"I'm lookin' for him."

"Why would a girl like you be lookin' for a bounty hunter?" he asked. "He bring in your old man or somethin'?"

"No," she said, "he *is* my old man."

He raised his white eyebrows in surprise.

"Really? Gavin Doyle's kid?"

She nodded.

"That's a big gun you got in your belt."

"It makes an impression."

"Why don't you have a seat?"

"Thanks."

She pulled a chair over and sat across from the old lawman.

"What's your name, kid?"

"Roxy Doyle."

"Well Roxy," he said, "your dad ain't been seen anywhere for years."

"I know it."

"Then why are you lookin' for him?"

"I'm his daughter. Isn't that reason enough? I've been lookin' for five years," she said. "I need to see him."

"And it would be best if he was alive for your little family reunion."

"Sure would."

"Then for your sake, I hope he is."

She nodded, stood up, started for the door, then stopped and turned.

"You've been a lawman for a long time."

He laughed. "How can you tell? Yeah, I been wearin' a badge in one place or another for more than thirty years."

"Did you ever meet my Pa?"

He studied her for a moment, and she thought he was trying to decide whether or not to tell her the truth.

"I met him once," he said.

"Where?"

"I was wearing a star in a town in Kansas . . . geez, I can't even remember the name. He came in with a bounty slung over his saddle."

"What happened?"

"I made sure he got paid."

She waited. "That's it?"

"That's it," he said. "I'm sorry I can't tell you more."

"Yeah," she said, "me, too."

She left the office.

Marshal Ira Dokes shook his head, picked up the posters and started leafing through them, again.

***

Back in the cell block Sam Abbott had listened with much interest to their entire conversation, and had found it very enlightening. He knew he was getting out of jail the next morning, so he settled back on his cot with his hands behind his head and a smile on his face.

Chapter Ten

Roxy didn't have much money. When she needed it she took an odd job in one town or another. She had just enough for a meal and a hotel for the night, so she could sleep in a bed.

She boarded her horse in a livery, took her saddlebags to a hotel and got a room. The clerk eyed her up and down, made her pay up front, then watched her walk up the stairs. He was old enough to be her father, but she knew what he was thinking.

Leaving her saddlebags in the room, she went out in search a place to eat. She found a small café that suited her, because it wasn't busy and didn't look too expensive. She had enough money for a bowl of beef stew, and a chunk of bread. The middle-aged waitress took pity on her and slipped her a second piece.

In the room she took the heavy Navy Colt from her belt and set it down on the bed next to her, then took her boots off and laid back without getting undressed.

She was asleep in minutes . . .

***

She woke late the next morning, which suited her just

fine. She had nowhere to go and nothing to do, not specifically. It would just be another day spent looking for her father.

She thought over her meeting with the local sheriff, and couldn't help feeling that he knew more than he was saying. He had been nice to her, gentle, treatment she wasn't used to. Maybe there was something he was going to tell her, and then he decided not to. Perhaps what she needed to do was go and see him again.

What she also needed to do was get some money. She didn't have any left, which meant she had to check out of the hotel. It was going to be necessary for her to get a job, and she had an idea about where to look.

She tucked the gun back into her belt and went downstairs, dropped the key off at the desk.

"So you got no money?" the clerk asked. It was the same one she had seen the night before.

"No," she said.

"But you need a room, right?"

"Yes."

He stared at her. "We can work somethin' out, you and me. Nobody has to know."

She knew exactly what he meant.

"No, thanks."

"Suit yerself," he said. "Just remember the offer."

She left the hotel without saying another word.

***

Marshal Dokes opened the cell door and said, "Okay, Abbott, time to go."

"Before breakfast?" the younger man asked.

"Go and get your own breakfast. Come on, get outta my jail."

"Okay, Marshal," Sam Abbott said, standing up and grabbing his hat.

He followed the Marshal out to the office, where the lawman opened a drawer and took out a gun and holster.

"There you go," he said, dropping them on the desk.

"Thanks, Marshal." Abbott picked up the gun and strapped it on.

"Keep yer nose clean, son," Dokes said. "I don't wanna see you in here again."

"Appreciate that, Marshal," Abbott said. "You have a nice day, now."

As Abbott went out the door, Dokes wondered what was going on. Normally, Abbott was belligerent and rude. Why was he all of a sudden being so polite?

Somethin' was up.

***

In front of the jail Sam Abbott grinned widely and stepped down onto the street. He needed to find his buddies, Ezekial and Tate. He had some news for them that they were going to find as interesting as he did.

***

Roxy entered the small café where she'd eaten the day before.

"Back so soon?" the waitress asked, smiling. "What'll you have this time?"

"No food," Roxy said. "I don't have any money. What I'd like is a job."

"Can you cook?" the woman asked.

"I used to," Roxy said, "but I haven't for a long time. I can wait tables, though."

"Why don't I have you cook me somethin', and then we'll see?"

"Well . . ."

She followed the woman into the kitchen, where she found a stove like she'd never seen before.

"I bought this and had it shipped here from the east," the woman said. "It's the newest thing in stoves."

Roxy looked at it and decided not to be intimidated by it. After all, a stove was a stove.

"What do you want me to cook for you?" she asked.

"Let's start with an egg," the woman said. "Any way you like."

"All right."

"My name is Maggie," the woman said. "My mother named me Magdalene, but I go by Maggie."

"My mother named me Roxanne," Roxy said, "but I go by Roxy."

"Okay, Roxy," Maggie said, "bring it out to me when you're done. The eggs are over there."

***

Several minutes later Roxy brought the egg out on a plate. She had made it into an omelet like she used to make when she lived in Salt Lake City with the Angelo family, adding some onions and peppers she also found in the kitchen.

After one bite Maggie said, "You're hired, and I'm puttin' this on the menu for breakfast today."

"Thanks," Roxy said.

"Let's talk about your pay."

"Whatever you say is fine," Roxy told her.

"Well then," Maggie said, "let's get you an apron."

Chapter Eleven

Three days into her new job, Roxy had cooked for the breakfast rush, then for lunch.

"I know you've been here all mornin' and afternoon," Maggie said, "but will you cook for supper? I'll pay you extra."

"Sure," Roxy said. "I can use the money."

"And just like with breakfast, you can eat for free."

Roxy had eaten with Maggie at breakfast, but had been too busy to eat lunch.

"That'll be great," she said. "I'll get ready for supper."

***

Sam Abbott had caught a glimpse from his cell of the girl in the sheriff's office. With that red hair, he figured she wasn't going to be hard to find.

"Are you sure she's Doyle's daughter?" Ezekial Moon had asked, when Abbott told him and Tate about the girl.

"That's what she said," Abbott answered. "Why would she say it if it wasn't true?"

"That sonofabitch," Tate said, "put my old man behind bars, and he died there."

"Did the same to my brother," Abbott said. "Now we have a chance to get revenge."

"On his daughter?" Ezekial asked.

"Why not?" Abbott asked. "Where the hell is Gavin Doyle now? Nobody knows."

"He may already be dead," Ezekial pointed out.

"Then this is our only chance at gettin' back at him," Tate said.

"Well," Ezekial said, "if you guys say so."

"We do!" Abbott said. "Now let's find her!"

And they spent the next three days trying to do just like . . .

***

Supper rush kept Roxy busy.

When she'd eaten there the day before, she had seen no sign that the place was this popular.

"The word's gone out that I have a new cook," Maggie told her, at one point. "That's why they're comin' in. And believe me, if the men in this town saw you, they'd be flockin' in even more."

"I'm just doin' the best I can," Roxy said.

"Well, I was doin' the cookin' before you got here," Maggie said, "and I didn't have people comin' in like this. So you just keep doin' what you're doin'."

Maggie kept bringing in orders and Roxy kept filled them as fast as she could. At one point she stuck her head out of the kitchen to ask Maggie a question, and that's when some of the men from town saw her. The word spread fast that not only was Maggie's new cook good, but she was beautiful.

And the word eventually got to the Devil's Own Saloon, where Abbott was drinking with Ezekial and Tate . . .

***

"Did you hear what I heard?" Abbott asked.

"About some cook in a café?" Tate asked. "What do we care?"

"Because," Abbott said, "they said that cook has red hair."

"You think it's her?" Ezekial asked.

"We been lookin' for her all this time," Abbott said. "II think we're gonna go and check it out."

They finished their beers and left the saloon.

***

"The handsome man at the far back table really likes his steak," Maggie told Roxy. "He wanted me to tell you."

"Handsome man?"

"Oh yeah," Maggie said. "He's my type, too. In fact, I think he's any girl's type."

Roxy went to the curtained doorway that separated the kitchen from the dining room, took a look at the man in question.

He was handsome, all right, in his thirties, working on his steak, but Roxy also noticed that he was watching the room. She'd seen men like that before, their eyes always darting around.

"See what I mean?" Maggie asked.

"He's either on the run," Roxy said, going back to the stove, "or he's huntin' someone."

"What makes you say that?"

"The way he watches the room," she answered.

"So maybe he's an outlaw?" Maggie said. "That would just make bein' with him more excitin'."

"He probably just wants to be left alone," Roxy said.

"You think so?" Maggie asked, touching her hair. "Maybe I'll just go and see if he wants anythin' else."

"Suit yourself, Maggie," Roxy said, and tossed another steak into the skillet.

***

Maggie was back in a few minutes. "Three men just came in, they all want steaks."

"Comin' up."

"They said they heard about the new cook," she went on, "and they wanted to know if she was as beautiful as they heard."

"Not if I was a good cook?"

"Well," Maggie said, "they're young men,"

This time Roxy wasn't interested enough to go to the door.

"I'll get them their suppers," she said.

"And the outlaw wants some strong coffee and a piece of pie," Maggie said. "I'll bring it out to him."

Roxy had made the coffee, but not the pie. That was Maggie's, from the day before. Roxy got busy preparing the meals for the three new customers.

Chapter Twelve

"Those three men," Maggie said, coming into the kitchen, "they want to give their compliments to the chef."

"What?"

"You know," Maggie said, "the three steak dinners? I didn't think they were the type, but they want to pay you a compliment."

"I don't know . . ."

"Oh, come on," Maggie sad. "If you're nice to them maybe they'll come back."

"Nice to them?"

"Oh, don't be like that, dear," the older woman said. "I just meant smile and accept the compliment."

"Oh, all right."

They went to the doorway together and Maggie pointed out the three men. Roxy noticed the handsome man in the back was still there, as well.

Roxy walked across the room to the table where the three men sat with their empty plates.

"You gentlemen wanted to talk to me?" she asked.

"We do if you're the cook," one said.

"I am."

Another man asked, "You're also Gavin Doyle's daughter, ain'tcha?"

Roxy froze. Her gun was in the kitchen, and all three of these men had theirs strapped to their hips.

"What are you talkin' about?" she asked.

The first man looked annoyed that the second man had spoken. He said, "I was in the jail when you talked to the sheriff. I heard ya."

"So?"

"Tate and me, we got a bone to pick with your old man."

"So?" she said. "What's that got to do with me."

"Well," the man said, "we can't find *him*, but we found you."

"I haven't seen my father in years."

"We don't care," the man said. "Like I said, we can't find him, but we found you."

"I think you should leave," she said, and started to go back to the kitchen.

The first man grabbed her wrist. "I don't think so."

"Let me go!" she snapped.

Maggie came to the kitchen door, saw what was happening. "Hey!" she yelled.

"Stay out of this!" the second man shouted back.

The third man remained quiet, looking around the room.

And then the handsome man was there.

"Let her go!" he said, coming up next to Roxy.

"You stay out of this, too," the second man ordered.

"I don't think so," the handsome man said. "Let go of her wrist."

The first man stared at him, then released his grip.

"You're makin' a mistake," he said.

"You made yours first," the handsome man said. "Now get out. All three of you."

The second man seemed to want to resist, but the first man stood up, and signaled the other two to follow him.

"This ain't over," the first man said to Roxy.

He and his friends left.

Maggie came running over to Roxy's side.

"Gee, thanks," she said to the man.

"Yes," Roxy said, "thank you for your help."

"My pleasure," the man said.

"My name's Maggie," "and this here's Roxy."

"Nice to meet you both," he said. "My name's Clint Adams."

"Really?" Maggie asked.

"Can I pay my check?" he asked.

"Oh no," Maggie said, "it's on the house, because of your help."

"Yes," Roxy said, "that's only fair."

"Well, thank you," Adams said. "You're a very good cook, young lady."

"Thanks."

"If you don't mind me asking," he added, "was what they said true? That you're Gavin Doyle's daughter?"

She hesitated, then said, "Yes."

"Your father's been out of circulation for a long time."

"I know," she said, "and I've been lookin' for him for a long time."

"And so have those men," Adams said. "Will you be all right?"

"I'll be fine," she said. "I can take care of myself."

"Are you sure?"

"I'm fine, Mr. Adams. Thanks."

Roxy went back to the kitchen.

"She's very young," he said to Maggie.

"Yes, she is," Maggie agreed.

"Well, I better get going." He walked to his table and got his hat.

"Come back and eat again," she said, as he passed her on his way to the door. "On the house, again."

"Thanks," he said. "I'll keep it in mind."

She watched him walk out the door, checked on her other customers, then went back to the kitchen.

"Do you know who that was?" she asked.

"Who?" Roxy asked, from the stove.

"Clint Adams," Maggie said. "Don't you know who he is?"

"The name sounds familiar, but . . ."

"He's the Gunsmith!" Maggie said.

"The Gunsmith?" Roxy repeated, in surprise. "Oh, my God. That's why the name was familiar."

"The Gunsmith ate here!" Maggie said. "That could put my place on the map!"

"Maggie," Roxy said, "I don't think he'd want you spreadin' that around. Not if you want him to come back."

Maggie bit her lip. "You're probably right."

"Let's finish up for the night," Roxy said.

"I'll collect from the last of the customers," Maggie said.

"I'll clean up in here."

"The Gunsmith," Maggie said, shaking her head. "Imagine that."

Chapter Thirteen

When Maggie walked back into the kitchen she said, "That's it. The last customer is gone."

"And I'm finished cleanin' up in here," Roxy said. "Good night, Maggie."

"'night, Roxy. See you tomorrow. Don't forget it's pay day."

"I won't forget."

Roxy grabbed the Navy Colt and tucked it into her belt, then walked through the dining room and out the front door. It was dusk, because Maggie didn't stay open late. She was about to step onto the street when a voice called out.

"Just stop right there, missy!"

She froze, turned her head. The three men from earlier stood there. She turned to face them, her heart beating a little faster, her mouth dry.

"Hey, Sam," one said, "lookee there, she's got a gun."

"A big one!" Sam Abbott said. "Sure you can handle that big gun, missy?"

"I can handle it," she said, although she certainly didn't think she could outgun three men. They had an audience, but she didn't see anyone who would step up to help her.

"Well, let's find out," Sam Abbott said. "What do you think your Papa will say when he hears about this?"

"Well," she answered, "since a lot of people think he's dead, he probably won't, so what's the point?"

"The point," Tate said, "is that we got a score to settle. With him, or with you, it don't make no never mind."

The third man was still quiet, but he stood with the other two.

"This isn't fair," Roxy said.

"Life ain't fair, missy," Abbott said, "but we'll let you draw your big gun, first. How does that sound?"

"I've got a better idea," a man said from behind her. Before she knew it, Clint Adams was standing by her side. "Why don't we even things up a bit?"

"How did you—" she started.

"I had a feeling these three wouldn't quit so easy," he said to her. "Are you ready?"

"I'm ready now," she said.

"You're askin' for it, Mister," Abbott said.

"Why don't you just shut up and get to it," Adams said.

With that the three men went for their guns.

The Gunsmith drew cleanly, fired twice, killing Abbott and Tate before they could clear leather.

Roxy pulled the Navy Colt from her belt, held it two-handed and fired, hitting the third man—Ezekial—in the shoulder, knocking him down.

She cocked the hammer, preparing to fire again, but Adams said, "No, wait."

"Why?"

"I don't think his heart was really in it. Besides, he can talk to the law for you, explain what happened."

He walked over to the fallen man, kicked his gun, which was lying in the dirt, away.

"That right?"

"Sure, sure," Ezekial said, "I'll talk to the law. I didn't have a stake in this like they did."

"That's good," Adams said. "You just saved your life."

"And you saved me," Roxy said to him. "Thank you."

"You know," Adams said to her, "if you're going to get into more scrapes like this one, you'll need a smaller gun."

Chapter Fourteen

The gunfight on the street made the Abilene newspapers. The report said that the Gunsmith, Clint Adams, outdrew three men, killing two of them, with the help of a red-haired beauty. One paper asked if she was a "lady" Gunsmith?

Roxy read the report the next day, and ran to the café to tell Maggie she would be in late.

"Why?"

"I have to find where Clint Adams is stayin'," she said. "I have to talk to him."

"Talk?" Maggie asked. "Well, you go ahead, girl, but try to make it back for lunch."

"I will."

"Oh," Maggie said, "and here's your pay."

Roxy accepted the money, pocketed it, and then went on her search, which would involve checking Abilene's many hotels.

***

She found him at the fourth hotel she checked. She was lucky enough to walk into the lobby of the Abilene House, where she saw him eating breakfast in their dining room.

As she approached his table people's heads turned to watch her, but she paid them no mind.

"Well, good-morning," he said, as she reached him.

"'mornin'."

"To what do I owe this pleasure?"

"I need to talk to you."

"If it's about yesterday, I was glad to help—"

"It's about more than that."

"Okay, then," he said, "sit down and have a cup of coffee. Although it's not as good as yours. In fact, have you eaten?"

"No, I haven't."

Clint called the waiter over. "Bacon-and-eggs okay?" he asked Roxy.

"It's fine." She actually was very hungry, and wouldn't mind eating food that someone else cooked.

He poured her a cup of coffee and asked, "What's on your mind?" while they waited for her breakfast to arrive.

"I need your help."

"With what?"

"I'm lookin' for my father," she said. "I've been lookin' for five years."

"I don't have any idea where Doyle is," he told her.

"Did you know him?"

"I met him once or twice, but I can't say I knew him."

"Well," she said, "I don't need your help findin' him, I need your help stayin' alive."

"Uh-huh," Clint said. "And just how would that work?"

"You said yesterday that I need a smaller gun."

"Yes," he said, "one that fits your hand."

"Can you help me find one?"

He chewed the bacon in his mouth, swallowed it and said, "Yeah, I could probably do that."

66

"And could you help me learn to use it?"

"Teach you to shoot?" he asked. "You didn't do too badly yesterday, even if the gun was too big and heavy for you."

"No," she said, "I can shoot. I've been able to hit what I shoot at since I was thirteen. But I've never worn a holster. I need your help getting a gun that fits me, and learning to use it—to draw it."

"Now look," he said, "I'm not in the habit of training would-be gunfighters—"

"That's not what I'm after," she said. "You helped me last night, but have you read the papers this morning?"

"Actually, no, I haven't yet. Are they covering it?"

"Oh, yeah," she said, "and they're callin' me Lady Gunsmith."

He stopped eating. "Are they really?"

"Yeah," she said, "and you know what'll happen if that name sticks."

"I have a good idea."

"I'm gonna have to learn to defend myself," she said, "and for more reasons than I'm used to."

"And what reasons are those?"

"The way I look," she said. "Men think they can . . . well . . ."

He waved at her and said, "Okay, I know what men think. Lady Gunsmith, huh?"

"If I can't defend myself," she said, "I'm as good as dead."

The waiter came with her breakfast and set it down in front of her. Clint waited for him to leave before speaking again.

"I was going to leave Abilene today," he said.

"I could leave with you, Mr. Adams."

"You can call me Clint, but anyway, you have a job."

"I just did that to pick up some money," she said. "It wasn't meant to be permanent. I want to leave, too."

He sipped some coffee and thought.

"All right, here's what I'll do," he said. "I'll go with you to buy a gun and holster that fits you. That'll keep me here one more day. Then we'll leave, and you can ride with me while I teach you to use it. But after that we have to split up."

"I have no problem with that, Mr. Adams, I mean, Clint," she said.

"Do you have a horse?" he asked.

"I do."

"Okay, then," he said, "eat your breakfast and we'll get started."

"I have to tell Maggie I'm quittin'," she said, "but I should work the day for her."

He gave it some more thought.

"Okay," he said, "you do that. I'll buy the gun and holster. I'll come by your café later for supper, and we'll talk. Then we'll probably leave town tomorrow."

"With my new gun!"

"Not until I know that you can shoot," he said. "And I also want to see your horse. You'll get the gun once we're on the trail."

"But—"

"And no buts," he said, cutting her off. "If you're going to ride with me, you'll have to do what I say, or our deal is off."

"Okay, Mr. Adams," she said. "We have a deal."

"Fine," he said, "now eat your breakfast, and forget that Mister business, just call me Clint."

Chapter Fifteen

Roxy's present . .

Kingman, AZ

The Number Two was lively that night. Lamps flickered, illuminating painted girls, dressed in bright colored satin and lace. Music from a piano that had been brought in from the East mingled with conversations. It was an excellent instrument, and even the off notes that were being hit by the second class piano player sounded clean and clear.

Roxy was standing at the bar with a beer, Jake working behind it, paying more attention to her than to all his other customers, combined.

The customers, on the other hand, many of whom had been present the night before when she gunned down two men, were still eyeing her. But along with approval there was no respect. No one had approached her with so much as a snide look, let alone an off-color offer.

It was her first beer of the night and she nursed it. She wondered if she would have handled the two men from the night before differently if she hadn't been into her third beer?

Sheriff Gifford stuck his head in, at one point, and then approached her at the bar.

"Plannin' on shootin' anybody tonight, Miss Doyle?" he asked.

"I don't know, Sheriff," she said. "I guess you'd have to ask these men if any of them plan on doing something stupid."

"That'd be a waste of time," he said. "Likkered up men are always ready to do somethin' stupid."

"I have to agree with you there," she said. "And speaking of likkered up men, can I buy you a drink?"

"I'm makin my rounds, Miss Doyle," he said. "I like to be sober when I do that."

"Well, then, come back when you're off duty, and I'll still buy you a drink."

"I'll keep that in mind." He touched the brim of his hat—not a move that looked comfortable for him—and said, "Ma'am?"

As the sheriff left, Jake the bartender came to the bar behind her and asked, "Givin' you a hard time?"

"Just doin' his job, Jake."

"Speakin' of doin' my job, you want another?"

"I'm fine," she said, showing him her still half full mug.

"What about after work tonight?" he asked. "We, uh, gonna repeat what we did last night?"

"I don't know, Jake," she said. "I'll have to see how tired I am."

"If you're too tired I can always do most of the work, you know."

She turned and looked at him. "I said I'd let you know, Jake."

"Yeah, okay," he said, "sure, sure. I ain't pushin'."

But most men did push. Usually, she was with a man once and moved on, so that they didn't get possessive, or expect anything. Jake was going to have to learn that the hard way.

Sometime later, she was about to ask Jake for a second beer, when three men came through the flap. They were all wearing trail clothes, but since the clothes weren't covered with dust, and two of them looked freshly shaved, she assumed they had ridden in earlier in the day.

The man in the center fit the description of Harlow to a "T".

She put her empty mug down and watched.

Of course, their first move would be to come to the bar.

"Beers," one of them said to Jake. The other one glanced over at Roxy, then looked away and said something to the man she figured was Harlow.

"Comin' up," Jake said.

He set beers down in front of the three men, then gave Roxy a sideways glance. She hoped he wasn't about to do something stupid, like try to help her. But men didn't necessarily have to be all likkered up to be stupid. Sometimes they just had to be men.

"What brings you gents to town?" he asked.

"Beer," said the one who had ordered.

"Well," Jake said, "I got plenty of that. I just thought there might be somethin' else—"

"Go away," Harlow said.

Jake frowned. "What?"

"You served us our beer, now go away. Don't come back unless I call you. Got it?"

"Yeah, sure," Jake said, "I got it. I was just tryin' to be friendly, is all."

"What I came to town to do is none of your business," Harlow said, "but I sure as shit didn't come to town to make friends. Now . . . go!"

Jake moved on down the bar to serve other customers, without looking over at Roxy. He was obviously embarrassed.

Now Harlow looked over at her, said something to the man who had already sized her up.

That man walked over to her, as she figured one of them would.

"Mr. Harlow would like you to join him for a drink," he said.

"He's got plenty of saloon girls to pick from."

"He don't want a saloon girl," the man said. "He wants you."

"Why?"

"He thinks you're interestin'."

"Is he interesting?"

The man laughed. "I guess you'll have to find that out for yourself."

Roxy made him wait a few moments, then shrugged and said, "Why not?"

The man led her down the bar to where Harlow and the other man were standing. Some of the customers standing at the bar gave them room. Undoubtedly, Harlow thought it was

73

out of respect for him, but Roxy knew different. Harlow gave a loud bark of a laugh at something his men said, then turned.

"I'm Jed Harlow," he said.

"Pleased to meet you," she said. "I'm Roxy."

"What are you drinkin', Roxy?" Harlow asked.

"Same as you."

"Bartender!" Harlow yelled.

Jake appeared.

"Beer for the lady."

"Sure."

Jake put a beer on the bar for Roxy but, didn't look at her, and then moved on.

"Thanks," Roxy said, and picked it up.

"Me and my boys, we're camped outside of town," Harlow said. "It's kinda cozy. Why don't you come on out?"

"With the three of you?" she asked.

"Well," Harlow said, "you could start with me." He laughed.

"I guess that'll depend on whether or not you've got what I want," Roxy said.

"Believe me, honey," Harlow said, "I got what you want."

"So that means you can tell me where Gavin Doyle is?"

Harlow frowned, not sure he heard right. "What?"

"The bounty hunter, Gavin Doyle," she said. "A man in Wichita told me you knew where he is."

"Doyle?" Harlow asked. "Lady, he's dead."

"That's what I heard," she said, "but I don't believe it."

"Why not?"

"Because I'm his daughter, and I'd know if he was dead."

"Look," Harlow said, "I don't know who you talked to in Wichita—wait a minute. Were you here waitin' for me?"

"For two days," she said. "Now that you're here, I want the truth."

"Lady I told you, Doyle is dead."

"How can you be so sure?"

"Because I saw it," he said. "I saw Gavin Doyle die."

Chapter Sixteen

"You're a liar!" Roxy snapped.

"Hey, girlie," one of the other men said, "watch who yer callin' a liar!"

"I'm callin' him a liar," she said, pointing at Harlow. "He's a goddamned liar!"

"Take it easy, Missy," Harlow said. "You said you were here lookin' for me, you wanted news about Gavin Doyle. So I told you what I know. He's dead."

"How?" she asked. "Where?"

"Ellsworth," Harlow said. "He was playin' poker and somebody shot him for cheatin'. I was there. I saw it."

"Now I know you're a liar!" Roxy snarled. "My Pa didn't gamble. Not on nothing. And he sure as hell didn't play poker."

"Maybe not when you knew him," Harlow said, "when you was a little girl, but men change."

"That's where you're wrong, Harlow," she said. "Men don't change. Not men like my Pa, and not men like you."

Harlow narrowed his eyes. "What's that mean?"

"You're a lair, pure and simple," she said.

Harlow's face grew red as he stared at Roxy. Then, suddenly, he seemed to calm down.

"Okay, fine," he said, "I'm a liar. If that's what you wanna believe, go ahead. It don't make no never mind to me." He turned to the bar, leaned on it and contemplated his beer.

"Harlow," one of the other men said. "You can't let her get away with that. Callin' you a liar."

"Relax, Miller," Harlow said. "She's just a girl."

Miller moved closer to Harlow and said something to him that no one could hear. Harlow listened, turned his head to examine Roxy a little more closely. He looked at everything, including the turquoise hat band.

Roxy was angry, but she didn't know what to do. She couldn't very well shoot Harlow for believing her father was dead. On the other hand, he could have been lying about seeing him killed.

Harlow nodded to Miller, then turned to face Roxy, again.

"You ain't asked who killed him," he said.

"That's because I don't believe he's dead," she said, "but who do you say killed him?"

Harlow shrugged. "A stranger. I never found out his name. For that you'll have to go to Ellsworth and talk to the local law."

"When do you say this happened?"

"Years ago, girl," he said. "You were probably still doin' laundry for whatever family raised you."

"What makes you think somebody other than my Pa raised me?" Roxy asked.

"Because your old man was makin' a name for himself when you were still wearin' . . . whatever little girls wear. He was too damn busy to raise you."

"What about my Ma?"

"She was dead before your Pa."

For Harlow to know that, he must have either known Gavin Doyle, or at least talked to him.

"Now, if you're who Miller thinks you are, we don't wanna shoot up the inside of this saloon, do we? Especially not after I jus' helped you out."

"Helped me?" she asked. "You pointed me towards Ellsworth. You really think I'm going to ride there on your say so?"

Harlow smiled. "Seems to me that's what you been doin' for a long time, girl, ridin' around here and there on other folks say so."

He was right. She'd investigated any scrap of information regarding her father's whereabouts. And if he really was killed, somebody in Ellsworth would know. And if he wasn't, well, somebody would know that, too.

"Now jus' say thank you and have a beer with us," Harlow suggested.

"I won't drink with you," she said, "but I'll say thank you for telling me what you think you know."

"What I think—" Harlow stopped short and laughed. "Okay, girlie, you just go to Ellsworth. You'll find out all you wanna know there."

He turned back to his beer, and his two partners did the same.

She still wasn't sure she believed him, but what could she do? Draw her gun and make him say something different?

She turned to the bar, stood there staring at the dirty, pitted wood on top.

"That wasn't what you wanted to hear, huh?"

She turned, saw Sheriff Gifford standing there.

"What are you doing here?" she asked.

"I heard some hard lookin' strangers rode in," he said. "I've been watchin' them. When they came in here, I had a feelin' you'd be involved."

"I just wanted to talk," she said. "I didn't shoot anybody."

"And for that I'm grateful. Can I buy you a drink?"

"No, thanks," she said. "I've had enough."

"Then is there anythin' else I can do to help you?" he asked.

"No—yes," she said, correcting herself. "I'm hungry. Do you know where I can get something to eat this late?"

"There's a place a few streets down," he said. "They won't have much, just some hardboiled eggs or sandwiches."

"What is it, a restaurant of some kind?"

"More like . . . well, a cantina, if it was in Mexico. Here I guess you'd call it a small . . . café. Beer, wine, coffee and, if you're lucky, a few morsels of food."

"I'll try it, then," she said. "Thanks."

"Sorry," Gifford commented, "guess you didn't find out what you wanted."

"I learned out what that man knows," Roxy said, "or what he thinks he knows. If I find out he's lying, he's not the kind of man who will be hard to find, again. Especially now that I've met him."

Chapter Seventeen

Abilene, KS
1875

Before leaving Abilene, Clint took Roxy to a gun shop and bought her a .36 Colt Paterson.

"It doesn't look that much smaller than the Navy Colt," she commented. "In fact, the barrel looks longer."

"It'll be lighter in your hand, fit your palm better," he assured her, "and I'm going to cut down the barrel. Right now it's seven and a half inches long. It has a range of 50 yards. I don't think you need that. I've always been more concerned with close-up work and accuracy."

"Well," she said, "if that's what you're concerned with, who am I to say different?"

They bought the gun, and a new leather holster for it.

"So, can I strap it on?" she asked, before they left the shop.

"Not yet," he said. "There's work to be done."

"What about this?" she asked touching the Navy Colt in her belt.

"We'll put that in your saddlebag, for now."

Outside, they went to their animals. Clint didn't object to her pony, though he did say she'd need a new horse at some point. This one would never be able to keep up with his big black gelding, Duke.

But for now, both horses were tied to the back of his wagon, which contained the tools of his trade.

"'The Gunsmith' is not just a name," he explained. "I also have the skills, though I don't use them very much, anymore. At some point I'll be giving up this wagon, and it may be soon."

It also said GUNSMITHING on the wooden side of the converted Conestoga wagon.

"And," he added, "you need new clothes."

"I don't have money for clothes, let alone a new horse," she complained.

"The horse will come later," he said, "but the clothes will be on me." He held up his hand to belay any complaint she was going to offer. "Let's consider it part of your training. I want you to approach your gun with a different attitude. Part of that is dressing differently."

"All right," she said, "I guess I'm in your hands." She looked alarmed at what she had just said. "I mean—"

"I know what you mean, Roxy," he said. "Look, if you don't trust me then you're not going to want to be alone on the trail with me. I can't have you worrying that I'm going to do anything to hurt you."

"I'm just used to men who . . . want their way," she explained.

"Well, yeah," he said, "I want my way, too, but I know I'm not always going to get it. And as for you, always be sure to get things your way. Remember, this was your idea, not mine."

"You're right," she said. "Okay, then, let's go shopping."

***

Abilene was a big town, and you didn't have to shop for clothes in the mercantile if you didn't want to. There were stores that specialized in women's clothes.

"Wow," she said, as they entered, "I've never been in a store like this before."

"There are still jeans and shirts, if that's what you want," he said, "but they're cut for women. It's time you stopped wearing men's clothes, that are too baggy for you."

For just a few moments, she looked at the dresses hanging on racks, but then they moved on and bought her shirts, jeans, boots, and a new wide, flat-brimmed hat.

She had a turquoise hatband on her old one, which was handed down from her mother. It was actually a necklace she wore all the time, but Roxy had turned it into a hatband because she wanted to keep it close.

There was a room in the back of the store where she could change, and when she came out she looked like a completely new girl.

"You look great!" he said. "Everything fits."

"Om my god," she said, staring into a mirror, "I look so different."

"You look lovely," the female clerk told her. She was a middle-aged woman wearing an expertly fitted dress, who had every hair in place. "I don't get many girls in here as beautiful as you. Are you sure you wouldn't want a few dresses? I'm sure your husband wouldn't mind."

"Oh," Roxy said, suddenly, embarrassed, "he ain't my husband."

The woman looked at Clint and touched her hair. Suddenly, her demeanor changed. "Well then . . . your brother, perhaps?"

"Just a family friend," Clint told the woman.

"I see." From that point on the woman was much more flirtatious with Clint. She was an attractive enough woman, and perhaps under other circumstances he might have been more receptive, but he kept to the task at hand.

Outside, they stowed the rest of her new clothes and the Navy Colt, in her saddlebags while people passing by paused to take a second and third look at the new Roxy Doyle.

"I feel like I should've taken a bath before putting on these new duds," she said.

"Don't worry about it," he said. "We're heading out, now. Somewhere along the way we'll find a stream or lake or some place for you to bathe."

"Along the way to *where*?" she asked.

He mounted up, left her to mount on her own, and said, "Between here and there."

Chapter Eighteen

They camped the first night near a stream that was not deep enough to bathe in, but Roxy was able to wash up thoroughly, and Clint left her to it while he took care of the horses, and built the fire.

She came back, drying her hair on a towel he'd given her from his wagon, and saw him sawing at her gun.

"How much are you cutting off?" she asked.

"About two and a half inches," he said. "I'm not turning this into a belly gun, I just want you to be able to get it out of your holster faster. And this'll make it a little lighter and easier to handle."

She sat down by the fire and set aside the towel.

"The coffee should be ready," he said. "Have a cup. We'll make supper when I'm done here."

"I'll pour you some coffee," she said, "and make supper. It's the least I can do."

"That'd be great," he said. "You'll find the fixings in the wagon. Make whatever you want."

She poured him a cup of coffee and set it down where he could reach it, then went to his wagon.

"Wow," she said, looking in the back, "are you sure this ain't a chuck wagon?"

"I just like to have a variety when I'm on the trail," he said. "Guess I'll be giving that up, too, when I give up the wagon."

"Why give it up at all?" she asked.

"Well," he said, "it's kind of asking for trouble these days for me to be riding around in a wagon with GUNSMITH painted on it."

"So paint over it."

"It also makes me too easy a target," he went on. "I can't move very fast in it. It's a concession to this reputation I have to carry around with me."

"You can't change that?"

"You'll find out," he said, "now that the newspapers have found you, that they don't give up on a story that easily."

She pulled a big pot out of the wagon, and all the fixings she needed to make a beef stew. By the time it was ready Clint had finished cutting the barrel of the gun down, taken the weapon apart, cleaned it, put it back together again, and loaded it.

"When can I shoot it?" she asked.

"Tomorrow you can start wearing it," he said. "After a few days, when it starts to feel natural, I'll have you shoot it."

"Really?" she asked. "I can't just shoot it tomorrow?"

"This gun is going to become part of you, Roxy," he said. "It'll go everywhere you go. It'll be within reach when you're eating, taking a bath, or sleeping. And you're never going to aim it."

"What?" she asked. "I can't aim the gun?"

"You'll point it, like your finger," he said, "and you'll hit anything you can point it at."

"I didn't think so much went into carrying a gun."

"Only if you want to carry it for a very long time."

He hefted the gun, cocked it and uncocked it, twirled it a few times to test the balance, then put it aside and accepted a plate of stew from Roxy.

"This is good," he said, tasting it. "How did you learn how to cook this?"

"From my mother, when we were on the wagon train," she said.

"Where's your mother now?"

"She was killed on the train by Indians," she said. "My father and me, we continued on toward Salt Lake City, but he never got there. He left me with another family, and went off to make money. At least that's what he told me. But I just think he didn't want to live a Mormon life in Salt Lake City. It was my mother who was the Mormon. After she died my father decided not to finish the trip, and he left me."

"But with a family, right?"

"A family that mistreated me, until I left when I was fifteen," she said. "He used to send money, and he came back to see me once or twice, but then the money stopped, and he never came back, again."

"And you don't believe the word that he's dead," Clint said.

"No, I don't," she said. "So I keep lookin' for him."

"Well, I hope you find him."

"With your help," she said, "maybe I'll stay alive long enough to do that."

Clint finished his stew and accepted another helping.

"I'm sorry," she said. "I didn't mean to dump all my troubles on you."

"That's okay," he said. "I think you needed to get some things off your chest."

"I thought I left all of that behind me," she said. "After all, I left five years ago, but I guess it's still in there. I think you're right, I needed to say it out loud."

"Tell me something, Roxy," he said. "And don't get mad at me for asking."

"I won't," she said. "Go ahead, ask."

"What makes you think you're father's still alive?"

She gave the question some thought. "I don't know for sure. I just think if he was dead I'd . . . feel it. Don't you ever think that way, that somethin' just doesn't feel right?"

"All the time," he said. "If I didn't pay attention to what I was feeling, I'd've been dead a long time ago. Those are your instincts, and you've got to follow them."

She pointed across the fire at him and said, with feeling, "Exactly! I gotta follow them, and they're tellin' me he ain't dead."

"Well then, by all means," Clint said, "keep looking."

"Thank you," she said. "I think I needed to hear that, too, and not just from anybody, but from someone like you."

"I'm glad I could help," he said. "You want me to help you clean up?"

"No, I got it," she insisted.

"Okay then," he said, "I'm going to check on the horses."

He made sure Roxy's pony and the two team horses were secure, then went over to Duke, who was standing very still, even though he wasn't tied.

87

"Listen good, old buddy," he said, stroking the big gelding's neck. "If anyone comes near the camp, raise the alarm. There was no way Duke would ever wander off.

By the time he got back to the fire, Roxy was wrapped in her bedroll and breathing deeply, fast asleep. He noticed the gunbelt was rolled up and placed right beside her, within easy reach.

She was a fast learner.

Chapter Nineteen

They rode all day the next day, with Roxy wearing the gunbelt, getting used to the weight on her hip. When they camped again she automatically went about building the fire and starting to cook. Clint took care of the wagon, and the horses. When he came back to the fire she handed him a cup of coffee.

"Supper'll be ready in a minute."

"No beef stew, tonight?"

"Somethin' simpler," she said, stirring the beans. "When do I get to shoot?"

"Probably tomorrow."

"Probably?"

"We'll see what happens. You never know what a day is going to bring."

"You're right about that," she said, thinking back to the day her mother died. That morning they never expected the prolonged Indian attacks, or that last, fatal arrow seeming to come out of nowhere.

"What will you do if the name Lady Gunsmith doesn't stick?" he asked.

"I'm not gonna go around gunnin' people down," she said. "If it doesn't stick I'll do what I've been doin'. Travelin' and lookin'. If it does I just want to be able to defend myself. I have enough trouble with men wantin' to touch me or bed me without also havin' them want to shoot me."

"You ever think of cutting off all that red hair?" he asked. "Maybe doing something different so you don't stand out so much?"

"I thought about it," she said, "but why should I have to change who I am just because men are pigs and can't control themselves?"

"Good point."

"And what about you?" she asked.

"What about me?"

"Don't you want to take me to bed?"

He stared at her.

"Don't get carried away with yourself, Roxy," he said. "There are plenty of women I can take t bed without having to chase you."

"I'm sorry," she said. "It's just been . . . ever since I was thirteen . . . it started with a man who was supposed to be raisin' me, and a boy who was like a brother . . ."

"You don't have to explain yourself to me," he said. "You were obviously a beautiful kid, and now you're a beautiful woman. I can understand how that would come with problems. I'm sorry."

"You're probably one of the few decent men I've ever met, Clint," she said.

"Well," he said, "now you went and did it."

"Did what?"

"I'm *never* going to try to take you to bed now."

She smiled at him. "I'll try to live with the rejection."

***

The next morning, after breakfast, he said to her, "Let's do some shooting."

"Now?"

"Why not? Let's see what you've got."

There was another clearing near camp. Clint took the empty bean cans from the night before and set them up on a fallen log.

"Can you hit those?"

"They're not that far away."

"We're starting slow."

"With the new gun?"

"I've seen you shoot the Navy Colt," he said. "How are you with a rifle?"

"Good."

He went and got his Winchester and handed it to her.

"Hit both cans with only two shots."

She worked the lever, raised the rifle to her shoulder, fired, worked the lever, and fired again. Both cans jumped off the log.

"Okay, good," he said, taking the rifle and setting it aside, "but that's not what we're here for. That was just for my information."

He went and retrieved the cans, set them up again.

"Now do it again, with the Paterson."

"Should I draw and fire?"

"Have you ever done that before?"

"No, never."

"Then just take it out and fire."

She took the gun from her holster, cocked the hammer, fired, then did it again and fired. Both cans leaped off the log.

"Okay," he said. "Wait."

He moved the cans from ten yards to twenty. She hit them again. He told her to reload, then try at thirty yards.

"You're a natural," he said, joining her and leaving the cans on the ground. They were pretty chewed up by then, anyway.

"I've always been able to hit what I aim at," she said, "but this is different. I didn't think I'd hit the cans without aiming, but you're right. I'm just . . . pointing, like the gun's my finger."

"It's all coming natural to you, which is good," he said. "Now, unload the gun."

"Unload it? Why?"

"We're going to work on drawing the gun from the holster, and I don't want you shooting yourself in the foot or, worse, shooting me."

When the gun was unloaded he took it from her, checked under the hammer to be sure, then handed it back.

"Holster it," he said.

She did. He explained that it wasn't always the fastest man with the gun who stayed alive, but the one who was most accurate.

"You can get the gun out first, but if you miss, you're dead. So let's see how fast you are, first."

She had a problem grabbing for the gun, not getting a solid grip on it the first time.

"You're not going to grab for it," he said. "You're going to let your hand hang down next to the holster. Then you'll bring your hand up and grip the gun on the way up. That's it. Then as you grip it, use your thumb on the hammer. By the time you point the gun, it should be ready to fire. Too many people are in such a hurry to get it out and point it that only then do they try to cock it. By that time, they're dead."

He worked with her for an hour on simply drawing the gun, cocking it and having it ready to fire.

"Okay," he said, "you're very smooth. And the cutdown barrel is helping you get it out faster. If I had the time, I'd convert it to double action, but you've got it. Now let's load it."

She took the gun out, loaded it, then slid it back.

"Okay," he said, "let's start with something large. Instead of a can on the log, shoot the log."

"Draw and shoot?"

"Yes," he said. "I just want to see if you hit it."

She stood with her hand hanging down by her side.

"Breathe normally," he said. "Don't hold your breath and then snatch for the gun. Take a breath, draw, fire, and take another breath."

"Shoot between breaths?"

"Right."

"Okay."

"Whenever you're ready."

She stood, waited, breathed, drew and fired.

And missed.

"Damn."

"That's okay," Clint said. "Do it again. Keep your eye on the log."

She stood again, arm dangling, then brought it up grabbed the gun, cocked it, pointed and fired.

The bullet struck the log.

"Again," Clint said.

She did it again, hitting the log.

"Again."

Hit the log.

"Okay," he said. "Let's try this." He picked up one of the mangled cans, put it on the log.

"Try that."

She went through the motions, drew and fired.

Missed.

Didn't get mad.

Tried again.

Missed.

On the third try, she hit it.

"Okay," he said, "that's it."

"That's all?"

"For now," he said. "When we camp today we'll try some more. We've got to get moving."

"Should I keep it on?" she asked.

"Sure."

"Loaded?"

He smiled. "Definitely."

As they mounted up she said, "So what do you think?"

"Lady Gunsmith?" he said. "I think you'll be able to live up to the name."

Chapter Twenty

Roxy's present . . .

Ellsworth, KS

Ellsworth, Kansas was once considered the wickedest Cowtown in the West. Dodge City was first, Abilene the last, but Ellsworth was the worst. The Kansas Pacific Railroad had a cattle pen and a stop there. Two years earlier, Wild Bill Hickok had run for sheriff, and was defeated in Ellsworth.

But like Abilene, the closing of the Kansas Pacific meant that Ellsworth's wild Cowtown days were behind it. It had now settled down into more of a farming and ranching community.

The main street that Roxy rode down was quiet, and she reined in her horse in front of Joe Brennan's Saloon, once one of the wildest establishments in town. But as she entered, she found it as sleepy as the street outside, even though it was late afternoon.

The few men who were there perked up as she entered, and watched her walk to the bar.

"Well," the portly bartender said, "hello, little lady—"

"Don't," she said, holding up her hand to cut him off. "Just let me have a beer."

"Sure thing, Ma'am," he said, and set her up with a lukewarm mug of beer.

In her search for her father, Roxy had been in a lot of towns, and a lot of saloons. She'd had cold beer, flat beer, lukewarm beer, and never developed a taste for any of it. Beer was just a way to start a conversation with a bartender, because they knew everybody and everything.

"Doesn't look like there's much happening, here," Roxy said to the man, whose tired eyes were looking her over. He'd obviously been a bartender a long time. He was bald and weary looking, but she had brightened his day.

"What're you lookin for?" he asked.

"Not much," she said. "I heard there were some big poker games hereabouts."

The bartender laughed. "Maybe in the old days, but not no more."

"Big names used to play here?"

"Well, yeah," he said. "Bat Masterson, Doc Holliday, Luke Short, they all used to come to town."

"Did they play in this room?" she asked.

"Yep," he said, "Joe's was the place to be back then."

She sipped the beer, managed to hide her distaste.

"Must've been some wild nights in those says," she said. "Were you here?"

He nodded. "For a lot of years. I seen a lot of things."

"Shoot-outs?"

"Oh, yeah." He leaned over a bit to look at the gun on her hip. "Seems to me that'd be somethin' you'd be interested in."

"Sure," she said, "if you've got stories."

"Lemme get you another beer," he said. "A fresh one."

He grabbed the one in front of her before she could respond, dumped it, and brought her another. This one had a good head on it, and was obviously cold, as the mug was frosty.

"That's good," she said, tasting it.

"Thought you'd like it," he said, smiling for the first time. "You know, if I was younger, I'd be doin' more than just tellin' you stories."

"Come on," she said, "you ain't that old."

"Well," he said, "I ain't feelin' as old as I was before you come in here, that's for sure."

Roxy graced him with a smile, and the man started talking . . .

***

She was in the saloon for over an hour, listening to stories about men named Masterson, Earp, Luke Short, Jim Miller, Ben Thompson and some lawmen called the Four Jacks— "Brocky Jack," "High-Low Jack," "Long Jack," and "Happy Jack."

She listened to all his stories, feigning interest, hoping that one would come up featuring her father, but the name Gavin Doyle never came up, so she decided she had to bring it up herself.

"All these stories are fascinating," she said. "But I heard one, maybe you can help me with."

"Sure thing," he said. "Just name it, sweetie." They had become much more friendly during the storytelling time—at least, that's what the bartender, Henry, thought.

"I heard Ellsworth is where Gavin Doyle was shot and killed during a poker game."

"That so?"

"Yeah, I heard he was shot by someone who came up behind him while he was playing."

"Honey," he said, "if a bounty hunter like Gavin Doyle had ever come to Ellsworth, I woulda heard about it. And that story? Sounds more like what happened to Wild Bill Hickok in Deadwood."

"So Doyle was never here?"

"Not to my recollection," he said, "but I'll tell you who was here—"

"I gotta go, Henry," she said. "Thanks for the beer, and the stories."

"But I got more!"

"I'll come back for them," she promised, although she had no intention of doing so. "Who's the law in this town now?"

"Charlie Brown's the law now," he said. "We ain't got a police department no more. That went away with the railroad."

"I'm much obliged, Henry."

"You come back here anytime, honey," he said. "You brightened an old man's day."

She looked around the empty saloon before she left, thought that it probably wouldn't have taken much to do that for the old barkeep.

***

Roxy rode past the boarded up, deserted building that at one time housed the Ellsworth Police Department. There had been a need for it when the cowmen came to town to blow off steam after a cattle drive. When thieves and pickpockets came to work the saloons and cow palaces. Especially when gunfighters and gamblers came to frequent the saloons and dance halls, and the prostitutes were working the saloons and streets. But like Henry had told her, those days were long gone.

She made her way to the old sheriff's office, and tied her roan to the hitching post out front. Then she mounted the boardwalk and entered the office. As she opened the door, it hung on one hinge.

"Careful there," the man with the badge called out, "might come off in your hand."

"Sorry," she said, closing it carefully behind her.

"Ain't your fault," the tall, gangly looking man said, "I been meanin' to fix it." He had a coffee pot in one hand and a cup in the other. "Coffee?"

"I could use it," she admitted.

"Then have a seat, little lady," he said. "I ain't seen anythin' as pretty as you since Prairie Rose was here, years ago."

Roxy sat and he handed her a full cup. Then poured another for himself and sat behind his desk. He was in his 40's, but appeared as tired and worn out as Henry and the town did. She supposed that was what came from living in Ellsworth for so long.

"Now what kin I do for you?" he asked. "What brings you to here?"

"I'm looking to confirm a story I heard."

"Well," he said, "we got lots of stories. Wasn't long ago this town was jumpin', but now the jumpin's done and all we got is stories. Whose was yours about?"

"Gavin Doyle."

"The bounty hunter?"

"That's right."

"I heard he was dead."

"That's what I'm trying to confirm."

"Now why would a pretty thing like you care about a dead bounty hunter?"

"Because he's my father."

The sheriff gulped down his mouthful of coffee and sat up straight.

"I guess I shoulda figured that when you walked in here wearin' that gun and that turquoise hatband. You're the one they call Lady Gunsmith!"

"My hatband?" She reached up and touched her Mama's necklace.

"It's one of the things folks identify you by," he said.

"Well," she said, lowering her hand, "my name's Roxy Doyle and that's what I answer to."

100

"We don't want no trouble in this town, Miss Doyle," he said. "Fact is, Ellsworth ain't really worth any trouble, anymore."

"I'm not looking for trouble," Roxy said. "I'm looking for my father."

"You think he's alive?"

She hesitated. "I feel he's alive. I want to confirm whether or not he's dead."

"Why come here?"

"I told you," she said. "I heard a story about him being killed here during a poker game."

"When?"

"Does it matter?" she asked. "Do you know anything about it?"

"Well," he said, "I've been the law here for a couple of years, and it didn't happen in my time. And I never heard anythin' about it happening during the so-called 'wild days.'"

"Who else is still living here from those days?" Roxy asked.

"Quite a few people," he said. "Some folks won't give up on Ellsworth."

"I need names."

"I don't think you're gonna get anythin'—"

"I'd like to ask," she said. "That's all I want to do. Ask questions."

"Miss Doyle—"

"And then I'll leave town," she promised.

The sheriff sat forward, took out a slip of paper and a pencil and wrote for a few moments.

"Here are four names, and where you can find them. I can't guarantee they'll even talk to you."

"Thank you," she said, taking the paper and standing up. "I'll take care of that part, myself."

Chapter Twenty-One

Since she had four people to talk to—at least—she put her horse up at the livery and got a room. She went to the Grand Central Hotel on the corner of Lincoln, once a favorite of the cattle barons and gamblers who came to town. Now they were happy to have a guest in their establishment.

She left her saddlebags and rifle in her room, and since the Grand Central's dining room was closed, asked the clerk where to go to eat. He directed her down the street to a café, where she got a bowl of beef stew that was palatable.

While she waited for her pie she picked her hat up from one of the other chairs at the table and looked at the necklace that acted as a hatband. She had no idea people might identify her by that it. Yet there was no way she'd be rid of it. It was all she had of her mother. She put the hat back down as her pie and coffee came.

After paying her bill she stepped out onto the boardwalk. It was dusk. She had the piece of paper in her hand with four names on it. Three of them were men who had businesses in town that would probably be closed now. The fourth was a woman with a business, and the address was right near where she was standing. She decided to walk by a have a look. She might get lucky.

***

Roxy ended up walking a couple of blocks. The store she stopped in front of had a big crystal ball painted on it, surrounded by painted hands, and the words FORTUNE TELLER above and below.

Fortune Teller?

And it was still open.

She shrugged, figured, why not?, and walked in.

There were curtains covering the walls, a round table in the center of a small room, with two chairs at it. A crystal ball rested on the table. A bell jingled when she closed the door. Immediately, a woman wearing a large, flowing dress that almost made her blend in with the curtains, came through the doorway.

"Hello, my dear," she said. "I've been waiting for you." She spoke with some kind of accent Roxy couldn't identify. But Roxy had seen a fortune teller in a circus once, years ago, and it sounded the same.

"You have?" she asked. "How did you know I was here? Or that I'd come?"

"The spirits told me," the woman said.

Roxy knew the woman was wearing a wig, and she had more face paint than a saloon girl or whore. She could have been forty or sixty.

"Please," she said, "have a seat."

"Are you Helga Graham?" Roxy asked.

"I am Madame Helga, yes," the woman said.

"The sheriff gave me your name—"

"Sit," Madame Helga said, "if you wish to speak with me."

Helga sat down and waited, so Roxy sat across from her.

"Now you may speak," Madame Helga said.

"The sheriff gave me your name, said you've lived here for a long time."

"That is true."

"Then maybe you can answer a question for me."

"I have the answers to many questions," the fortune teller said.

"Good, I need—"

". . . for a price."

Roxy stopped and stared at her. The woman interested her, so she asked, "How much?"

"One dollar . . ."

"That's not too ba—"

". . . per question."

"That's kind of steep."

Madame Helga spread her hands. "These are hard times. You've seen that the streets of Ellsworth are not exactly teeming with potential clients."

"Yeah, I've noticed."

"It is why I stay open so late," Helga said. "I must be available when the need strikes—like your need."

"And you know what my need is?"

"But of course," Helga said. "You need to commune with one who has passed."

"You can talk to the dead?" Roxy asked.

Helga smiled and held out her hand. "One dollar."

Chapter Twenty-Two

"I'll give you two-bits a question," Roxy said.

Madame Helga closed her hand, but left it out there.

"You wish to bargain with the fates?"

"Two-bits."

Madame Helga thought a moment, then said. "Four bits."

Now it was Roxy's turn to consider. "All right, four bits."

Helga opened her hand.

"Keep a running tally," Roxy said.

Madame Helga raised an eyebrow, then withdrew her hand.

"Very well," she said. "Ask."

"You can talk to the dead?"

"I commune with the dead," Helga said. "They speak to me. Who do you wish to commune with?"

"First, do you know who Gavin Doyle is."

"Of course I do."

"Tell me."

"But you know."

"Humor me."

Madame Helga sighed. "Doyle is an infamous bounty hunter, well known for bringing his prey in dead, not alive."

"The word is out that Doyle was killed here, in Ellsworth, while playing poker. You've lived here a long time. What do you know about that?"

"You are asking me to use my memory," she said, "not my powers. That will still be four bits."

"Agreed."

"I never heard anything about Gavin Doyle being in Ellsworth," she said, "and I've lived here for over ten years."

"He never even passed through?"

"Masterson, Earp, Luke Short, many of the infamous . . . not Doyle. Not while I've been here. Maybe before?"

"No," Roxy said, "not before."

"Then no," Madame Helga said. "Now, ask me something I can use my powers to answer for you."

"Is he alive, or dead?" Roxy asked.

"The bounty hunter? Why do you want to know?"

"He's my father."

"Ah!" Helga said. "Now we get to it." She put both her hands out. "Take my hands."

One of the things she'd learned from Clint Adams was that her gunhand must always be free.

"I can't—" she started.

"If he is dead, we will find out," Helga said. "Take my hands."

Roxy rubbed her palms on her thighs, then reached out and took Helga's hands. The woman didn't tighten her fingers, as if she was going to hold onto Roxy so somebody could bushwhack her. She held them lightly.

Madame Helga fell silent, rubbed Roxy's palms with her thumb, closed her eyes, waited . . . then released Roxy's hands and sat back abruptly.

"What is it?" Roxy asked.

"Nothing," Helga said. "There is nothing."

"What do you mean, nothing?"

"No messages," Helga said, "no presence from the other side."

"So you're saying my father isn't dead?"

"That is what I'm saying," Helga replied. "I feel no presence in the afterlife of Gavin Doyle."

Now Roxy fell silent.

"Does this surprise you?" Helga asked.

"No," Roxy said, "I felt he wasn't dead."

"And now I feel it."

Roxy stood up. She gave more credence to the woman's memory than she did her so-called powers.

"Thank you for your help."

"There is the matter of my payment?"

They did the math, settled on the price, and Roxy paid Madame Helga.

"You can come back here any time," Helga said.

"I won't be in town much longer," Roxy said. "I just have a few more people to talk to."

"Perhaps someone's memory will be better than mine," Helga said. "Or . . . different."

"Maybe," Roxy said.

Madame Helga smiled at her.

"Thank you," the fortune teller said.

"For what?"

"I know what people think of me," Helga said. "I have been in this business a long time. I have worked in carnivals and circuses, before I opened this storefront during the wild days. I have been accused many times of being a fake. You have been very kind, and I hope I have been of some help to you."

"You have," Roxy said. "And whether or not you're a fake doesn't concern me."

Helga frowned at her. "You have had a hard life."

"Lots of people have."

"You sound educated."

"I had schooling," Roxy said, "but for years now I've educated myself, changed the way I talk and think. There's no need to sound stupid if you can avoid it."

Helga laughed. "My dear, the one thing I can tell about you just from this short meeting is, you are not stupid."

"Thank you."

"But you must be warned, my dear," Helga said. "There are dark days ahead. There is a man who is not who he says he is, and there are those who will always try to harm you, even kill you."

"That's been my situation for the past few years, Madame Helga," Roxy said, "but thank you for the warning."

Chapter Twenty-Three

Hays, Kansas
1875

When Roxy Doyle rode into Hays with Clint Adams, they had been on the trail for five days. Five days of getting to know her new gun, feeling at home with the weapon in her hand and the holster on her hip. She had come to the point that when she drew the gun and fired it, she hit what she was pointing at, every time.

When they camped the night before, Clint had told her, "We're going to part company in Hays."

"Why?"

"Because I've shown you all I can," he said. "The rest is up to you."

They were planning to have a drink and a farewell meal together, first. He didn't say where he'd be going, and she didn't know where she'd was headed. Just that she'd be continuing her search for her father, better equipped to handle whatever came her way.

They reined in their horses in front of the Jack of Clubs Saloon, and dismounted.

"You're going to see the inside of a lot of saloons during your search," he said.

"I already have."

"Well," he said, "there's going to be more of everything. Saloons, livery stables, hotels, and towns. It'll get monotonous. But it's going to be necessary as you continue your search."

"For my father."

"And you're going to find something else."

"What's that?"

"Trouble."

"I've already found a lot of that, too."

"I'm sure that's the case, but you're better equipped to handle yourself now. But when it does come along, you have to do whatever it takes to avoid it, walk away from it. And if you can't, when push comes to shove, trust your instincts."

"Thanks to you, I know I'll be fine."

"Not me," he said. "I'm sorry about the name, though. *That's* on me."

***

It was early, and when they entered the Jack of Clubs not much of anything was happening. As was always the case for the both of them, they drew attention. With Roxy, it was because of who she was, what she looked like. It was because of the red hair. For Clint Adams, it was because of the way he carried himself. Men knew that he was not a man to be crossed.

Roxy and Clint eyed the three or four men seated at tables with drinks, discounted any of them as an immediate threat, and walked to the bar. The two men standing there watched, then looked away.

The bartender, a big, heavy man with forearms like tree trunks, waited for them to say what they wanted.

"Two beers," Clint said.

"I don't usually serve girls," the man said.

"You'll serve this one," Clint ordered.

He looked the man in his eyes, and the bartender averted his gaze, fetched two beers, set them down and walked away.

"I'm for a steak after this," Clint said, picking his up.

"Beef stew for me," she said.

"Is that a thing for you?"

"My mother used to make the best beef stew," Roxy said.

"Yours is pretty good." Clint heard some horses stop out-side.

"I guess I'm lookin' to find one that'll taste like hers," she said.

"So you're searching for more than one thing."

"I suppose so."

At that moment a noisy group of five men stumbled through the batwing doors, laughing and slapping each other on the back. From the condition of their trail clothes, Clint assumed these were the men who had just ridden in.

"Five beers!" one of them yelled at the bartender.'

"Whiskey!" another shouted. "We ran out of whiskey on the trail."

"Which is it," the bartender asked, "beer or whiskey?"

"Both," one said, as the five of them made their way to the bar. "We're celebratin'."

"Whataya celebratin'?" the bartender asked, setting up the whiskey and beer glasses.

"None of your damned business!" they all said, and started laughing.

Then one of them looked down the bar and saw Roxy.

"Oh my," he said, "would you look at that."

All five men turned, their eyes glassy with rotgut shine.

"See?" the bartender said to Clint, after he'd finished filling the glasses for the five men. "This is why I don't serve girls in here."

"Don't worry about it," Clint said.

"Hey, honey," one of the men said, "you got room for five more?"

"We're just havin' one beer and then we'll be on our way," she said to him.

"Aw, don't be like that, darlin'," another man said. "We're jus' lookin' to have some fun."

"I'm sure there are plenty of girls in town lookin' for fun, boys," she said. "I'm just not one of them."

"You too good fer us?" another asked. "Is that it?"

"Yeah, that's it," one of his friends said, "she's too good for us."

Roxy looked at Clint, her expression saying, See what I go through?

"Okay, fellas," Clint said, "you can have your fun without botherin' the lady. Why don't we buy you all a round before we take our leave?"

"Who's talkin' to you, friend?" one of them asked.

All of the men were young and drunk, which was a bad combination. It didn't look as if any of them were over thirty, just a few years younger than Clint.

"Why don't you just be on your way and we'll take care of the lady," another said.

Clint was losing track of who was saying what. They all had the same drunken cadence to their voices. And they all wore guns. Drunk young men with guns always spelled trouble, and all he wanted was to get Roxy out of there before it started.

"I think we're done here," he said, putting his beer mug down.

As he and Roxy turned to leave, three of the men moved between them and the door.

"Hey, look there," the one by the bar said. "The girl has a gun."

"You need that to protect your man, honey?" the other man by the bar asked.

"He don't need my protection," Roxy said, "believe me."

"So you need his?"

"I can take care of myself," she said, "especially against a bunch of sloppy drunks."

"Sloppy?" one asked. "Did she call us sloppy?"

"Hey look," Clint said, "you fellas are drunk and you're making a bad move, here."

"Hey," one of the men blocking the way out said, "we was just tryin' to be nice."

"Okay," Clint said, "let us be nice and buy you a round of drinks and be on our way."

"Nuh-uh," one said. "Nope. We want you to go and leave the lady here."

"She's too pretty for you," one of the others said. "We're gonna show her what it's like to be with some real men." He slapped the flat of his hand on the bar. "Up here, girl. We're gonna take turns showin' you what it's like to be with real men."

"Okay, that's enough!" Clint snapped. "Nobody's touching her."

"Last of all you idiots," Roxy added. "You wouldn't know a real man if he bit you on the ass."

It got very quiet in the saloon. The few other patrons quickly got to their feet and looked for cover. The bartender froze behind the bar.

One of the drunks said to him, "If you go for a shotgun under that bar, I'll kill you first."

The bartender raised his hands and backed away, bumping into whiskey bottles behind him, knocking a couple to the floor, where they shattered.

"You got one choice, Mister," one of the men blocking the door said. "Walk out the door, or go for your gun."

That was it. Now there was no way for Clint to walk away. He knew it, and Roxy knew it.

"The girl can move out of the way," one of the men by the bar said. "We don't want her gettin' hurt."

"We'll still have use for you, darlin', after we kill your boyfriend," the second man by the bar said.

Chapter Twenty-Four

"I'm not goin' anywhere," Roxy said.

She looked at Clint, whose eyes flicked over to the two men standing by the bar. She nodded her understanding. He would take the three men blocking the door, the two at the bar were hers.

"This has almost gone too far, boys," Clint said, "but nobody's dead, yet. And there's no reason for anybody to die, not over a silly argument."

"You tryin' to talk your way outta this?" one man by the bar asked. "You don't know who you're dealin' with, here."

"You heard of the Dawkins gang?" another asked.

Shit!

Clint had heard of the Dawkins gang. So had Roxy. Two of them were brothers, and the others were gang members they'd grown up with. At a young age they had gained reputations for robbing trains and banks.

"I didn't know you boys were in Kansas," Clint said.

"We're aimin' to take Kansas for all its worth," one of them said.

"Which one are you?" Clint asked.

"I'm Luke Dawkins," the one by the bar said. He indicated the man standing next to him. "This is my brother, Abe."

"Who're you, friend?" Abe asked. "I'd like to know, before we kill ya."

"He's Clint Adams, that's who he is," Roxy said.

The three men blocking the door stirred, nudging each other.

"Who-eee," Luke Dawkins said. "We got us the Gunsmith here, boys." He looked at Clint. "You got yourself quite a reputation there, fella."

"Well," Clint said, "you know how reputations go. For instance, you boys have got a reputation for making stupid decisions."

"Like this one," Roxy said. Her heart was beating quickly, and her lips were dry. She was nervous. Five against two was not very good odds. But she was bolstered by the fact that Clint didn't seem nervous, at all.

Both Dawkins boys' eyes went very cold.

"Now, that ain't nice, Adams," Luke said. "I don't like bein' called stupid."

"But you are stupid, Luke," Clint said, "and you're even dumber when you're drunk."

"Luke," Abe said, "I don't like this fella. Or his bitch. I think we oughtta kill 'em both."

"Well," Luke said, "we gave the girl a chance to walk away, and she didn't take it."

"Your reputations are gonna take a big hit," Roxy said to them, "when the word gets out that you were killed by a girl."

Both Dawkins brothers had been leaning on the bar. Now they straightened up.

Clint took one step away from Roxy, to make more room between them. He wished the Dawkins brothers were in front of him blocking the door, and that Roxy was not standing

117

between him and them. Because of that, they were hers. He had been hoping that after the short period of training, it would be a long time before she had to use that new gun.

But it wasn't to be.

Chapter Twenty-Five

Clint Adams was confident enough in his own speed and ability with a gun that he watched Roxy, waiting for her to draw.

Roxy studied the two Dawkins brothers, counting on Clint to take care of the other three men who were only in her vision peripherally. When Luke and Abe Dawkins went for their guns, she moved.

Everything that Clint had taught her passed through her mind in seconds. She took a breath, drew her gun, and fired between breaths. Her first shot struck Luke square in the chest. Clint had told her that when she fired at a man, she should fire, dead center, at the largest part of him.

Luke grunted, his eyes opened in surprise, because his gun was not yet out of his holster. He only had time to register that fact before he died, even before he hit the floor.

Abe was clutching at his gun, in exactly the way Clint had told Roxy never to do. She cocked the hammer on her Paterson and fired again, also shooting Abe through the chest. The younger Dawkins brother had just enough time to start to cry before he collapsed to the floor next to his brother, dead.

Roxy was aware of three shots to her right, and as she turned with her gun, she saw that the other three members of the Dawkins gang were on the floor, dead.

"It's okay, Roxy," Clint said, putting his hand on her shoulder. "It's over. Eject the spent shells, reload, and put it away."

Only then did Roxy realize she had flown in the face of Clint's training. She had not taken her second breath. In fact, she had held the first.

She let the air out of her lungs, and did as he told her. Both of their guns were reloaded and holstered by the time the sheriff and his deputies burst through the batwing doors.

***

Roxy and Clint were taken to jail for questioning, but in the end, the sheriff returned their guns to them, having listened to their story, and the eye witness accounts from the bartender and other patrons.

"Doesn't seem they gave you much of a choice, Adams," Sheriff Gentry said to Clint.

"On the other hand," Clint said, "we gave them every chance to walk away, Sheriff."

"Yeah, I'm sure you did."

Standing to one side were Gentry's two young deputies. They had listened to the entire tale, but their eyes were glued to Roxy the whole time. She ignored their lovesick stares.

"Are you and the lady stayin' in town?" Gentry asked.

"Just overnight, Sheriff," Clint said. "We came here for a drink, a beer and a bed. That's it. We weren't looking for trouble."

"But it has a way of findin' you, doesn't it?"

"I'm afraid so."

Gentry looked at Roxy, who had strapped her gun back on and was waiting.

"You the little lady the newspapers in Abilene called Lady Gunsmith?"

"I'm the little lady," she said.

"I hope you folks don't mind me askin' you to leave town first thing in the mornin'," Gentry said. "We just don't want any more trouble here."

"Neither do we, Sheriff," Clint said. "You can depend on us leaving in the morning."

"Thank you. Uh, by the way, there was a bounty on the Dawkins boys. Not those other three, but on the brothers. You want that money, you can collect it here before you leave town."

"We don't want—" Roxy started

"The lady will take the money, Sheriff," Clint said, cutting her off.

"It'll be here."

They left the office, started across the street.

"I don't want no bounty money, Clint," Roxy said.

"You need a stake, Roxy," Clint said. "It's something you don't ever have to do again if you don't want to, but I suggest you take it this time, just to get yourself started."

Considering Clint had brought her the clothes on her back and the gun and holster on her hip, Roxy said, "Yeah, okay. I'll take it . . . this time."

"Now let's get something to eat."

Clint had his steak and Roxy her stew at a restaurant down the street from the sheriff's office. Apparently, word had already gotten around, for the stares they got were more intense, and tinged with a little more fear than usual.

"They think we're monsters," Roxy said, while they ate.

"Not monsters," Clint said. "We just did something they've only heard about, and none of them will ever experience in their every day lives. Don't let it affect your meal."

She tried to do as he said.

"My hands are still shakin'," she admitted.

"That's okay," he said. "I was hoping this day was a little further off for you, but you did fine. Killing is never easy, and you killed two men today."

"I killed men before," she said, "and those men deserved it. That ain't why my hands are shakin'. I was scared out of my mind."

"Nothing wrong with that," Clint said. "A good dose of fear is something to learn from."

She shoveled beef stew into her mouth, chewed and swallowed, then smiled.

"What's funny?" he asked.

"Sure doesn't seem to have affected my appetite."

Chapter Twenty-Six

After supper they went to their separate rooms, agreeing to meet in the morning for breakfast, then to pick up the bounty money from the sheriff.

Roxy sat on the bed, and waited as long as she could. As she got up, walked down the hall to Clint's room and knocked on his door. Her heart was beating even faster than it had in the saloon.

"Who is it?" Clint's called.

"It's me, Roxy."

He opened the door a crack, peered out, then opened it all the way. She saw the gun in his hand, held down by his side.

"You always answer the door with that gun in your hand?" she asked.

"You bet I do," he said, "and it's a habit you better get into, also. What's up?"

"I wanted to talk. Can I come in?"

"Sure." He backed away to let her in, walked to the bed-post and slid the gun back in the holster that was hanging there. She closed the door.

On the bed she saw a book.

"What are you reading?"

"Charles Dickens. I read him and Mark Twain a lot."

"I never read Dickens," she said, "but I have read Twain. 'The Jumping Frog of Calaveras County.'"

"A good one," he said. He sat on one side of the bed, his back to his gun. He was wearing his jeans, but was bare-chested and bare-foot. "Have a seat. What's on your mind, Roxy?"

She sat gingerly at the foot of the bed, her hands folded in her lap. She was still wearing her gun.

"Will I ever see you again after tomorrow?" she asked.

"I don't know," he said. "I hope so. Why?"

"I . . . I've kinda got used to you."

He smiled. "I've gotten used to you, too."

"How come . . ." she started, then stopped.

"What?"

"How come all those nights on the trail you never once . . . never tried . . ."

"To touch you?"

She nodded. "Yes."

"You've told me stories, Roxy," he said. "About the treatment you've gotten from men. I never wanted to be one of those men."

"But you're not!" she insisted. "I mean, you're not like any man I ever met, Clint."

"Roxy—"

"I'm twenty years old, Clint and I don't think I've ever been with a man I really wanted to be with."

"You just haven't met the right one."

"With you, it'd be different," she went on. "I can tell. You treat people . . . women . . . the way they're supposed to be treated."

"I treat women the way they deserve to be treated."

"You see?" she said. "What other man would say that?"

"Roxy," he replied, "I know what you're saying, here, and I want you to be sure."

"First of all," she said, "I have to know if you want me."

"I'd be an idiot not to," he said. "You're beautiful, you're sweet—"

"Sweet?" She laughed. "I've never been called sweet."

"—but you're a little damaged."

"Now you're just bein' nice," she said. "I'm a lot damaged, but I think I need time with someone I want to be with, and I've never met anyone I want to be with . . . until now."

She turned, got on her hands and knees on the mattress and crawled toward him.

"I don't know exactly what's ahead of me after we leave here," she said "but I do know one thing . . . I need this night."

She moved into a seated position beside him and leaned against him, with her face raised, hoping he'd give in.

And he did.

He kissed her. At first it was just a meeting of the lips, but then she opened her mouth and accepted his tongue. The kiss deepened, and went on for a long time. When they parted she was breathless, her heart still pounding.

"I knew it!" she said.

***

He was gentle.

She expected it, yet she couldn't believe how gentle.

He removed her gunbelt, hung it on the other end of the bedpost, so they'd both have easy access if they needed them. Then he undressed her, starting with her boots.

When he took off her shirt her large breasts fell into his hands. His thumbs found her nipples, and she bit her lip. Men had touched her nipples before, but only to pinch or twist them. Clint let his thumbs glide over them, teasing until they were hard as diamonds.

Then he began kissing her body, first her neck and shoulder, then the slopes of her breasts. He held them in his hands, cradling the heavy undersides, and his tongue touched her nipples.

"Oh God . . ." she groaned.

He smiled, licked her nipples some more, then bit them, but gently, just worrying them between his teeth. She put her hands on the back of his head and held him there a moment, then wrapped his hair in her fingers, pulling his head away so she could kiss him.

"You're drivin' me crazy," she said.

"I'm just enjoying you."

"Well," she said, "I'd like to enjoy you. Please, get those pants off."

"Now?"

"Yes," she said, "now!"

She watched as he stood up and slid off his pants and underwear. When his hard cock came into view she caught her breath. She'd seen ugly penises before—big, small, thick, skinny—and this was not one of them. This one was perfect, smooth, just the right length and thickness.

"Come here," she said, reaching out.

"No," he said.

"What?"

"We've sat around the campfire and talked, Roxy," he said. "You've told me about your experiences with men. Your foster father, your foster brother, other men you've encountered over the past five years, since leaving home."

"So?"

"You like to be in control," he said. "You need to be. You like to make men beg for what you give them."

"What's your point?" she asked.

"My point is," he said, "I'm not going to beg. I want you to lie back and relax." He moved closer, and she reached out to grasp his cock. He let her hold it for a moment, and then pushed her down on her back. Just for a moment she felt panic. Men had tried this before, pushing her down, then mounting her. But he didn't do that. He got on his knees, ran his hands up and down her thighs and legs, then began to kiss them. She tried to relax.

He kissed her thighs, her calves, ran his hands over them again and again. His hands moved up her body, then, over her belly and ribs until they were holding her breasts, thumbing her nipples, and then his face was between her legs. She spread her thighs to give him better access, and then his tongue was on her, in her, all over her. These sensations were new to her. It felt good, so good she couldn't believe it. This had to be real pleasure, and he seemed intent on showing it to her.

She felt something starting in her legs, a trembling, and as he continued to work on her with his mouth, his lips, his tongue, and his hands, she was finally able to give herself up to it. She closed her eyes and accepted the sensations, the pleasure, and for the moment, completely gave up control . . .

***

The night continued. Clint let her have her way, allowed her to explore his body, finally concentrating on his penis, stroking it, caressing it, licking it, and taking it into her mouth. She sucked him, and while he never begged, as he said he wouldn't. She could tell he enjoyed it. And she realized she was not only giving him pleasure, but taking some for herself, as well. Bringing him to the point where he exploded, giving him so much enjoyment, made her feel good.

Being with a man made her feel good, for a change . . .

***

Then Clint took her again, this time piercing her with his hard cock, and when he entered her she wanted to laugh and cry at the same time. She wrapped her legs around him, enjoyed how their bodies felt as they slapped together, as he glided in and out of her, at how wet she was and how hard he was—all of it.

This was how it was supposed to be between a man and a woman.

Finally.

PART TWO

Chapter Twenty-Seven

Roxy's present . . .

In five years' time Roxy's search had taken her from Kansas, all over the West, and right back to Kansas, again. Kansas was where she'd first been called Lady Gunsmith, it was where she met and trained with Clint Adams, and it was where she had killed the Dawkins Brothers, cementing her reputation as Lady Gunsmith.

Wichita, Abilene, Ellsworth, Hays . . . and now Coffeyville, Ks.

So much of who she was, the Lady Gunsmith part of who she was, which she had come to terms with and accepted with the help of Clint Adams, had happened in Kansas.

Where she went, what she did was not always about her father. After ten years, the rumors were coming fewer and further between, and now she was back in Kansas not to look for him, but passing through because she was on her way to Missouri. Why? She'd never been to Missouri.

Her time in Ellsworth, talking with some of the older residents, including the fortune teller, Madame Helga, had convinced her of one thing: her father had not died there. But she also had no clue where to look next.

Except for . . . Jed Harlow.

He'd sent her to Ellsworth on a fool's errand. And now, visiting Missouri because she'd never been there was not her only reason for stopping. Like she'd told the sheriff, Harlow would not be a hard man to find . . .

***

She rode into Coffeyville, her last stop in Kansas before crossing into Missouri. She knew that just a mile south was the Indian Territory, presided over by Hanging Judge Parker and his marshals.

After spending time in the formerly wild towns of Abilene and Ellsworth, Coffeyville was refreshing. The main street was busy with pedestrians, carriages, buckboards and horses traveling back and forth. It was a busy, thriving town.

So busy that the street took a beating. There were holes everywhere, some covered by boards until they could be filled. After riding hundreds of miles on the trail without a mishap, Roxy's roan stepped in a hole. She felt it as soon as the animal did, and dismounted immediately.

"Damn it!" she swore aloud. She bent to examine the hoof and leg. Nothing seemed broken, but the roan didn't want to put any weight on it.

"Bad luck."

She turned, saw a tall, handsome man of mixed blood standing in the middle of the street smiling at her. The smile was infectious, and she returned it in spite of herself.

"I know," she said. "All the trail we rode, and he steps in a hole as soon as I get to town."

"Looks like you'll need a vet and a livery," the man said. "Luckily we have both. I can show you where they are, if you like."

"That's real kind of you."

"No problem," he said. "I hate to see a horse suffer. My name's Sam."

"I'm Roxy."

"It's this way, Roxy," he said. "Just follow me."

***

She did as he asked, but did it warily, waiting for the other boot to fall. He could have been leading her into a trap, but eventually they came to a livery stable with a sign on the outside that read HOSTLER AND VET INSIDE.

"That's real handy," she said.

"It sure is," Sam said. "I think all towns should have 'em."

He opened the doors, swinging them aside, so they could walk in abreast, leading the horse.

"Dandy!" he shouted.

A man came from the back of the barn, wiping his hands on a dirty rag. He was in his forties like Sam, but taller and thinner and not nearly as handsome.

"Roxy, this here's Dandy Wallace," Sam said. "He's the town vet and hostler."

"I'm pleased to meet you, Miss," Dandy said. "Do you need to put your horse up for the night, or is there another problem?"

"Both," she said. "Stupid critter stepped in a hole as we got to town."

"That's Eighth Street," Dandy said, "it's full of holes. The town council keeps sayin' they're gonna do somethin' about it, but it never happens."

"And as long as they don't," Sam said, "you'll be gettin' a lot more business, won't you?"

"You got that right," Dandy said. "Let me have him, Miss. I'll unsaddle him, rub him down and check that leg."

"I'm much obliged," Roxy said. "I'll just take my saddlebags and rifle."

"I'll get 'em for you," Sam said, stepping forward.

He grabbed the bags and rifle, then handed the horse off to Dandy.

"Thank you," Roxy said, reaching for the bag.

"I'll take it for you," Sam said. "I assume you're gonna want a hotel?"

"Guess I'll need one," she admitted.

"Well, if you'll let me," Sam said, "I can lead you to that, too."

"Seems to me you're just as friendly as can be, ain't you?" she asked.

"I try," Sam said, "I surely do."

Chapter Twenty-Eight

Sam led Roxy to a hotel that was on that torn up Eighth Street, called ONION CREEK HOTEL. Roxy had crossed Onion Creek on the way in.

"It's got nice rooms, and a good dining room," Sam assured her, as they entered the lobby.

"Well," she said, "hopefully my horse isn't hurt too bad, and I won't need more than one night."

Sam frowned. "I was hopin' to have time to get to know you better."

"That so? We'll have to see. I can take those saddlebags now."

"You sure?" Sam asked. "I mean, I can carry them up to your room for ya."

"That's okay, Sam," Roxy said. "I can handle it from here. I'm obliged to you, though."

"All right, then," he said, and handed them over. Then he tipped his hat. "I hope to see you again real soon, Roxy."

She watched as he crossed the lobby and went out the front door. There was no denying he was a handsome man, but like she'd told him, she hoped to be in town only one night.

She checked into the hotel, deflected the comments of the young desk clerk, who was obviously smitten.

"Um, are you, uh, friends with Mr. Starr?" he asked, as he handed her the key.

"Who?"

"That was Sam Starr who brung you in here," the clerk said.

"Well," she said, "I just rode into town and met him. He helped me out when my horse stepped in a hole outside."

"Town council keeps sayin' they're gonna fix that street," the clerk said.

"That's what I hear," she said. "Thanks."

She went up the stairs and down the hall to her room, which did not overlook Eighth Street. There was no access from there, which suited her.

She used the pitcher-and-basin on the top of the dresser to wash some trail dust off her hands and face, then dried off, leaving her saddlebags and rifle in the room, and walked out. She ignored the clerk along the way.

Passing the dining room she saw that it was only about half full, but she needed to make one stop before she sat down to supper.

***

"Back already?" Dandy asked, as Roxy reentered the livery.

"Just wanted to let you know where I'm staying," she said. "The Onion Creek Hotel."

"Okay," he said. "I'm soakin' that roan's leg. When I know somethin' for sure, I'll send word."

"Thanks."

She walked back to the hotel, dodging people on the boardwalk and making sure she didn't step in any holes when she crossed the street. She didn't want to suffer the same fate as her roan.

As she entered the hotel dining room a man rushed to ask if he could help her.

"A table," she said. "I'm stayin' at the hotel."

"Of course, Ma'am," he said. "This way."

The man led her to a table which, to her surprise, already had an occupant.

Sam Starr.

"Your guest is here, sir," he said.

"Thanks, Walter," Starr said, standing. "Please, have a seat. I've been waiting for you to order."

Roxy stared at him and his disarming smile.

"What made you think I'd be here?"

"You just got to town," Starr said. "You must be hungry. So was I. I thought we'd eat together, get better acquainted."

"I'm intending to leave town tomorrow," she reminded him.

"All the more reason we should eat together tonight," he told her. "Sit?"

She hesitated a moment before saying, "All right. Thanks."

As she sat down another man, a waiter, appeared and anxiously rubbed his hands together.

"This is Stuart," Starr said. "Our waiter. I met him a couple of days ago, when I got to town. Just tell him what you want and he'll see that you get it."

She looked up at Stuart, a young man who was very eager to serve the lovely redhead.

"I'll have a steak, with everything."

"Yes, Ma'am. Mr. Starr? A steak for you?"

"Sure, Stuart. That sounds great."

"Right away!"

As Stuart left, Starr asked her, "Coffee?"

"Yes, thanks."

He poured her a cup, having already ordered a pot and two cups.

"So," Roxy said, "you're new to Coffeyville, too?"

"Well, I got here two days ago, but I've been here before," he said, "so no, not new."

"I can see why people would remember you."

"How's that?'

"Come on," she said. "You know you're charming and good-looking."

"I'm just glad you know it," he said, his smile widening. "What about you? Where are you headed?"

"Missouri."

"Why?"

"I've never been there before," she said. "I thought I'd go to St. Joe and see if I could meet Jesse James."

That surprised him.

"You really want to meet Jesse James?"

"No," she said, "I was just kidding. Why would I want to meet an outlaw?"

"Jesse's no outlaw," Starr aid. "He's a man with a mission."

"Tell that to the law," she said. "You know Jesse?"

"We've met."

"Are you friends?"

"Let's just say we've met, and leave it at that."

"Okay."

The waiter came with their food.

"How does it look?" he asked.

"Looks fine, Stuart," Starr said. "Thanks."

As he left, Roxy leaned forward. "That was fast. You had already ordered these, right?"

Sam Starr smiled. "I thought you'd have a pretty good appetite after riding a long way."

"How'd you know I rode a long way?"

"Your horse," Starr said. "He stepped in that hole because he was too tired to avoid it."

"You know a lot about horses?" she asked, picking up her knife and fork.

"I know a lot about a lot of things," he said. "Why don't we talk while we eat?"

***

It turned out Sam Starr had one major failing that Roxy could see. He was handsome and charming, but he also liked to talk about himself. And she had an idea that most of what he was saying was lies. So, he was like a lot of men, but the charm and good looks went a long way toward making it all bearable.

In the end, he turned out to be a pleasant enough supper partner for her . . .

Chapter Twenty-Nine

. . . and also a pleasant enough bed partner.

She wasn't sure when she'd decided to have sex with him. It could have been the moment they met, or the moment she saw him sitting at that table, waiting for her. In any case, after supper they went for a walk around town, still talking, and eventually—after dark—they ended up back in her room, and in bed.

Clint Adams had taught her that all men wouldn't deserve being made to beg for sex with her, and Sam Starr turned out to be one of those kind. She'd never met a man as giving as the Gunsmith was in bed, but Sam Starr was close. In the end, it turned out to be part of his charm. And, since they weren't talking while they were having sex, she didn't have to listen to his stories. It was just his charm, his good looks, and a pretty nice cock.

She woke the next morning with Starr lying on his stomach next to her. That was unusual. She usually made her bed partners leave as soon as they were finished.

She studied the back of his head, where his hair curled at his neck, the line of his back as if led down to his buttocks, which was covered with fine black hairs, as were his legs. But his chest had very few of them, and she had liked that. She had found him a tasty man, and she wasn't finished tasting. He woke while she was peppering his ass with light kisses.

"Now that's a helluva way to wake up," he said, into his pillow.

"Turn over," she invited him, "and I'll show you another way."

He didn't have to be asked twice.

***

"I think the whole hotel heard you, that time," she said, when she was done sucking him.

"Jesus," he said, "who cares? Wow!"

"But it's time to get up now," she said, slapping him on the thigh and then bounding out of bed. She knew he was watching as she walked nude to the pitcher-and-basin to clean herself.

"Good God, but you're a gorgeous woman, do you know that?"

"I do know it," she said.

"Well," he said, putting his hands behind his head, not moving from the bed, "you're not modest, are you?"

She turned her head and looked at him over her shoulder while he studied her ass.

"Do you know how many times I've been grabbed, groped, or almost raped because of the way I look?"

"Well, that ain't right," he said. "I hope you shot all those men."

"Some of them," she said,

She turned from the basin and began to get into her clothes. Starr still watched.

141

"I told you it's time to get up," she said, sitting on the end of the bed to pull on her boots.

When she stood up and turned she saw that he had taken her Paterson from the holster on the bedpost, and was pointing it at her.

"What if I don't wanna get up?" he asked.

***

Belle entered the sheriff's office, and the man looked up from his desk, not surprised. Concerned, but not surprised. He knew that Sam Starr was in town, and that he'd been seen in the company of a certain redhaired woman who had just arrived the day before. If Belle found out about that, there'd be hell to pay.

"Hello, Belle," he said, standing from behind his desk.

"Sit down, Glen," she said, waving him down. "I stopped bein' a lady a long time ago."

The sheriff sat.

"You seen Sam?"

"Around town," Sheriff Glen Marks admitted. "Ain't seen him this mornin', though."

"I been lookin' for him for an hour," she said. "If you see him, tell him I'm at our hotel, eatin'. I rode all night to get here and I'm starved."

"I'll tell 'im," the sheriff promised.

"Thanks."

She left, and the sheriff stood up, put on his hat and gunbelt, and peered out the window. When he was sure she was gone, he went out and headed for the Onion Creek Hotel.

***

Starr twirled the gun and held it out to Roxy, butt first.

"Pretty light," he said.

"It suits me," she said, accepting it. She walked to the bedpost and retrieved the gunbelt. She felt like a fool, letting him get his hands on her weapon. This never would have happened to Clint Adams. She counted it as a lesson learned.

"I notice it's cut down," he said. "He do that for you? The Gunsmith?"

"That's right."

"I ain't never run across him," Starr said.

"You don't want to."

"He as good as they say he is?"

"Better." She strapped on the holster, slid the gun home.

"Best you ever seen?" Starr asked.

"By far."

"That'd be real interestin'," Starr said.

There was a hurried knock at the door and Roxy drew her gun.

"Who is it?" she called.

"Sheriff Marks! I'm lookin' for Sam Starr."

Roxy looked at Starr.

"It's okay," he said, swinging his feet to the floor. "He ain't lookin' to arrest me. We're friends." He grabbed his pants and slid them on. "Go ahead and let him in."

Roxy went to the door, gun in hand. She cracked it, looked out, then swung it open to reveal a tall, grey-haired man wearing a badge.

"Hello, Ma'am."

"Sheriff."

He looked past her, saw Sam standing by the bed.

"Aw, Shit, Sam!" he said.

"What is it?"

"She's here," he said. "She just got to town."

"Belle?"

Marks nodded.

"You tell her where I was?"

"Told her I seen you in town, but not this mornin'."

"Where is she, exactly?" Starr asked.

"In this hotel," Marks said. "Downstairs, eatin'."

"She seen you come in?"

"No, I snuck past her."

"Okay, Glen. Thanks."

"What're you gonna do?"

Sam Starr smiled. "I'm gonna go downstairs and have breakfast with my wife."

The sheriff looked at Roxy, then headed off down the hall. Roxy closed the door, swung around to face Sam Starr.

"Belle?" she snapped. "You're married to Belle Starr?"

"Well, yeah," he said, grabbing his shirt.

"Then what the hell are you doing sleeping with me?"

He shrugged. "I thought you knew."

She was tempted to shoot him, but holstered the gun.

"I should have," she admitted. "I didn't put it together. I don't know why." It was the second stupid thing she'd done involving Sam Starr.

He sat on the bed and pulled on his boots. "I do. She's Belle Starr. She's famous, like Lady Gunsmith is famous. Me? I'm Belle Starr's husband. Well known? Maybe around here, the territories, maybe Missouri, but famous? Not me."

"And you resent that?"

He didn't answer. Instead he said, "I gotta go have breakfast with her, but I'll see you later. Okay?"

"No!" she snapped. "Definitely not okay. You better get out of here, Sam."

"Okay, you're mad—"

"You think so?"

He approached her, and she backed away.

"I don't sleep with married men."

"Okay, well," he said, "ain't neither one of us gonna tell Belle about this, right?"

She hesitated, then decided to let him sweat.

"You go down and eat with your wife, Sam," she said, "and I'll think about it."

"She'd kill us both, Roxy, Lady Gunsmith or not."

"She'd kill *you*," Roxy said, "that much is for damn sure."

"Roxy—"

"Go!"

"Okay," he said, offering his hands in a placating gesture, "we'll talk later."

"Get out, Sam!"

He opened the door, then turned and gave her that charming smile. "I had a real good night, Roxy."

She put her hand on her gun and he slammed the door.

Chapter Thirty

Roxy decided to make Sam Starr sweat even more, and go downstairs for breakfast. She entered the dining room and saw him sitting with a dark haired, hard looking woman who was smiling. That sonofabitch! She was angry that he had hoodwinked her, that she had allowed him to slip past her defenses and spend the night only to discover that he was married to the Outlaw Queen. She should have shot him, but that would have caused a whole lot of trouble of another kind.

***

When Sam Starr approached his wife, Belle looked up at him and smiled.

"Where the hell have you been?" she asked, but her tone was sweet, as it was when she talked to him. Belle was completely enamored of her husband, had been since they first met. "I've been lookin' all over for you."

Sam leaned down, kissed his wife and then sat across from her.

"That's what Glen Marks told me," Sam said. "Believe it or not, I slept late."

"I pounded on the door."

"Well," he said, "I got kinda drunk last night. You shoulda came right in."

"Are you kiddin'?" she asked. "What if I found you there with some whore? I woulda had to kill you both!"

"Yeah, you would've," Sam said, "but believe me, I didn't have no whore in our room."

"You better not!" Thankfully, she was still smiling. Belle Starr was not a beautiful woman, but she was smart and tough, and a wildcat in bed. Sam Starr was very happy to have her as a wife, but he wasn't thrilled that she had been accepted as the head of the Starr gang.

"You order yet?" he asked. "I'm starved."

"Just now."

"Well," he said, smiling, "I'll have to catch up."

He waved a waiter over and gave him his order, then stopped short when he saw Roxy Doyle at the entrance to the dining room.

***

Roxy was shown to a table, attracting the usual amount of attention. As she sat she noticed that Belle Starr was looking over at her, the smile gone from her sour face. Sam wouldn't have told her, would he? No way would he do such a thing.

The waiter came and obstructed any further view of Belle Starr.

"Ham-and-eggs," she told the waiter, "and coffee."

"Yes, Ma'am."

She was surprised to see Belle Starr walking across the room toward her. Sam Starr sat staring, and when he saw Roxy looking at him, he just shrugged.

When Belle Starr reached her table Roxy looked up at her and waited.

"You're a very strikin' woman," Belle said.

"Well, thank you."

"I hope you don't mind," Belle said, "but are you the one they call Lady Gunsmith?"

"My name is Roxy Doyle, if that's what you're asking."

"I knew it." Belle actually smiled, then. "I knew there couldn't be two women who looked like you."

Roxy decided to play dumb.

"And who are you?"

"Well, you may have heard of me," Belle said. "I'm Belle Starr." She actually put her hand out.

Roxy took the hand, and shook it. "You're right, I have heard of you. I thought Judge Parker had his marshals chasing you all over the Indian Territory."

"Oh, he does," Belle said. "We come up here once in a while just to take a break. Say, my husband and me, we have a bigger table than you do. Would you join us for breakfast?"

Roxy looked over at Sam, who shook his head.

"Well, sure," Roxy said. "Why not?"

***

As Belle Starr led Roxy Doyle over to their table Sam

Starr's blood got colder. Either this was going to get very interesting, or turn into a bloody mess.

He smiled.

***

"Sam," Belle said, "I told you this was Lady Gunsmith." She looked at Roxy. "He told me he didn't think so."

"Well," Roxy said, looking at him, "you were wrong, weren't you?"

"I was," Sam said, standing. "It's a pleasure to meet you."

"Likewise," Roxy said, and shook Sam's hand.

"I asked Roxy to have breakfast with us, and she said yes. Ain't that nice?"

"Real nice," Sam said. "You ladies should sit."

They did, and he waited a second before seated himself.

Roxy could see from the look in Sam's eyes that he was worried she was going to tell Belle Starr where he spent the night. But she decided not to say a word about it, so he'd be worried sick through the whole meal. Maybe something would go down the wrong way and he'd choke.

"Well," Belle Starr said, "what brings the famous Lady Gunsmith to Coffeyville?"

"I guess the same thing that brings the famous Belle Starr here," Roxy said. "Just wanted to take some time off and relax a bit. Plus, when I rode into town my horse stepped in a hole, so I'm here whether I like it or not."

"I think you'll like it," she said. "Coffeyville's a friendly town. Ain't that right, Sam?"

Roxy spoke before Sam could. "I've already found that out. In fact, folks have been way more friendly than I could have hoped for."

Chapter Thirty-One

Over breakfast the two women chatted away while Sam Starr tried to eat, even though he felt like his throat was closing—like there was a noose around his neck.

"I had to walk over and meet you," Belle said. "There aren't that many women like us. You know, we can intimidate men just by lookin' at 'em. Now me, I do it because I'm so mean and deadly. But you, Jesus, you're beautiful and deadly!" She looked at her husband. "Ain't she beautiful, Sam?"

"Huh?" Sam looked up from his plate. "Oh, yeah, she sure is, hon."

"Oh, go back to your food." Belle looked at Roxy. "He's pretty, but he ain't that smart."

"Hey, wai—" Sam started to complain.

"I hope you don't mind me saying so," Roxy said to Belle, cutting him off, "but I could tell that just by looking at him."

"Yeah," Belle said, "smart men ain't easy to come by. Hey, you know Clint Adams, right? The Gunsmith? That's how you got the name?"

"He was real helpful to me."

"Is he smart? I mean, I heard he's good with the ladies, but I never heard nothin' about how smart he is."

"He's the smartest man I ever met," Roxy said.

"That's good," Belle said. "When you hear that much about a man, you want him to be the best he can be."

"Well, he is," Roxy said. "I can swear to that."

"So how long you plan on bein' in Coffeyville?" Belle asked.

"Just till I find out how my horse is," Roxy said.

"So you'll stay if your horse's hoof needs more tendin'?"

"Either that," Roxy said, "or I'll trade him for another horse."

"When are you gonna find out?" Belle asked.

"Probably this morning," Roxy said, "after breakfast. Why?"

"I was just thinkin'," Belle said, "if you was gonna be around a while, I might have a proposition for you."

"Well," Roxy said, "as soon as I find out, I'll be sure to let you know."

"That'd be good."

"Or," Roxy said, looking at Starr, "I could let Sam know."

"Huh? What?" Sam said.

"Never mind, honey," Belle said. "You just finish your breakfast and let the girls talk."

Roxy was starting to understand why Sam Starr had slept with her, and couldn't much blame him for it.

***

After breakfast the three of them walked out to the hotel lobby.

"I gotta get a bath," Belle said. "I rode all night to get here to see my Sam. I wanna be sweet smellin' for him."

"I'll get on over to the livery and check on my horse."

"You do that," Belle said, "and let me know as soon as you find out somethin'."

"I'll do that," Roxy said. "Thanks for breakfast."

"My pleasure," Belle said. She touched Sam's face. "You gonna wait for me upstairs, sweetie?"

"I'll be there when you get there," he promised.

Belle patted his cheek and walked off to arrange for her bath. Roxy noticed the gunbelt and gun on her hip were both well worn.

"She treats you like a puppy," Roxy said.

"Not all the time," Sam said, "but it does get tiresome."

"I'd think so."

"Thanks for not sayin' nothin'."

"Look," she said, "seein' the way she treats you, I don't much hold it against you, but it ain't going to happen again. You got that?"

"Yeah," Starr said, "I got it, Roxy. I better get on up to the room and wait for her."

"You do that."

Belle was gone from the lobby, so Roxy watched as Sam Starr walked across and went up the stairs. It was too bad his backbone didn't match that long, hard cock of his.

***

At the livery she found Dandy rubbing down a pretty looking Palomino pony.

"'mornin'," he greeted. "I was hopin' you'd drop by."

"Good news, or bad?" she asked.

"Bad, I'm afraid," Dandy said, straightening up. "Your roan has a strained tendon in his left foreleg."

"How bad?"

"It ain't torn," Dandy said, "that's the good news, but it'll take a while to heal."

"What's a while?"

"A few days, at least. Maybe a week."

"You got a horse I can trade for?"

"Not likely," Dandy said. "Right now I've no extra stock in my corral."

"What about this one?" Roxy asked, indicating the pretty Palomino.

"I wouldn't trade this fella for a roan with a strained tendon," the vet said.

"Can I buy him?"

"I doubt you could afford him," Dandy said, then added, "no offense."

"None taken," she said. "He does like look a piece of expensive horseflesh."

"He is."

"You own him?"

"No," he said, "this horse is owned by a gent who lives here in town."

"Uh-huh," Roxy said.

"And he ain't lookin' to sell."

Roxy stroked the Palomino's neck. "Anybody else in town got a horse to sell?"

"I don't know," Dandy said, "but I can ask around."

"I'd be obliged if you did," she said.

"I'll send word over to the Onion if I hear of one," he promised her.

"Thanks."

"You, uh, mind if I give you some advice before you go?" he asked.

"About what?"

"Sam Starr."

She waved a hand. "I'm way ahead of you. I just met and had breakfast with Belle and him."

"Ah, so he told you about Belle."

"He did not," she said, "but I heard."

"Then you know," Dandy said. "Belle killed the last girl she caught Sam with."

"I don't doubt it," Roxy said. "Well, Belle seems to like me, and I ain't about to risk my life just to be with Sam Starr, that's for sure."

"I'm glad to hear it," he said.

"But thanks for the warning."

"Any time."

She stroked the Palomino's neck again, then turned and walked out of the stable. Dandy watched her until she was out of sight, then went back to working on the pony.

Chapter Thirty-Two

Roxy wondered if Belle Starr's proposition to her was going to involve money? She also wondered if it would be legal. Probably not. Still, she needed some cash in order to continue on her way, or else she'd have to wait for the horse's tendon to heal.

On the other hand, she'd been riding a lot lately, mostly because of Harlow. Catching up to him somewhere in Missouri and getting him to admit he lied about Ellsworth didn't mean he was going to have some truth to tell her. Staying in one place for a week or so would give her some time to rest up, and get the roan back in shape. Then if Harlow was still in Missouri, so be it.

Since leaving Ellsworth, where the most interesting person she'd met had been the fortune teller, she hadn't heard anything about her Pa, Gavin Doyle. Maybe ten years was long enough to harbor the hope that he was still alive, or that she'd even find him.

So far the most interesting person she'd met in Coffeyville was Belle Starr. Maybe Belle was right. Maybe there weren't that many women around like the two of them, and they should spend some time together.

She reached her hotel, and decided to just keep on walking. Thinking about Belle and Sam Starr up in their room in bed wasn't pleasant for her. And she already knew from experience that Sam Starr was a loud lover. She didn't relish sitting in her room, listening to the sounds of their lovemaking down the hall.

So she just kept walking.

***

Sheriff Glen Marks stepped out of his office, and immediately spotted Lady Gunsmith walking on the boardwalk across the street. The woman was hard to miss, what with that red hair and the gun, let alone the way she walked. Men and women turned and watched as she went by, and Marks couldn't much blame them.

Sam Starr was at the same time a lucky man for having bedded her, and a dead man if Belle Starr found out. He wondered just how long Roxy Doyle and Belle Starr were going to be in his town. He could already smell the fuse burning down . . .

***

Roxy found what she wanted a few streets down from her hotel, a saloon that was small and almost empty. She just wanted to sit and lean over a beer without anybody leering at her, or trying to make her acquaintance. She even liked how bored the heavyset bartender looked as she approached.

"Beer," she said.

"Sure thing."

She looked around and saw that every table was empty.

"How long will it stay like this?" she asked, as he set the beer in front of her.

He sighed. "Most of the day."

"Suits me." She picked up the mug and headed for a table.

"Glad it suits somebody," he said, behind her.

***

Sam Starr ran his mouth and hands over his wife's sweet smelling skin. She was still warm from her bath, and her hair was wet. Her breasts were smaller than Roxy's, her nipples dark brown as opposed to the lighter color of Lady Gunsmith's. Belle Starr was a plain woman, and when Sam was in bed with her, he often compared her to other women he had been with. He knew it wasn't fair, but there it was. And now that he'd been with Roxy Doyle, he'd be comparing all women to her, especially Belle Starr.

"My baby," Belle said, cradling his hard cock in her hands. She rubbed it along her cheek, brushed her lips over it. This was the only time he ever really saw a tender side to his wife, the Bandit Queen. "My sweet baby," she said, and took his penis into her hands.

"Oh yeah." Belle climbed aboard her man, sitting astride him in a position of power. She lifted her hips and took his cock deep inside of her, then began to ride him. Sam Starr knew better than to try and flip her over. Belle always liked to be in charge, in bed and out . . .

***

Roxy nursed her beer, thought about the last ten years, the last few months, about her father, and about Jed Harlow.

She blamed Harlow for making her waste time getting to Ellsworth, asking questions there. But maybe it wasn't his fault. Going back through her thoughts, maybe it was the fault of the person who had sent her after Jed Harlow. But if she was going to start second guessing herself now, then why not second-guess the whole last ten years?

She couldn't do that. If she did, she was lost.

Chapter Thirty-Three

"What's this about making this Lady Gunsmith an offer?" Sam Starr asked.

Belle, lying next to him, made circles with her hand on her own belly, staring at the ceiling while the sweat dried on their bodies.

"We're waitin' for the rest of the gang to get here, right?" she asked.

"Yeah, so?"

"Wouldn't she make a good addition to the gang?"

"You're crazy."

"Why?"

"Have you ever heard anythin' about her pullin' jobs?" Starr asked. "Bein' wanted?"

"I've heard about her bein' a fast gun." Belle said. "You see how young she is? And already she's got a big reputation."

"She ain't that much younger than you."

"You're sweet, but yeah, she is, five or six years younger," Belle said. "She's still got time to build that rep, make it even bigger. Can you think of a better way for her to build it than to team up with me?"

Starr noticed that Belle said "me," not "us."

"She'll never go for it."

"You let me worry about that," Belle said. "I'll get her to go for it."

Now Starr put his hands behind his head and said, confidently, "Ain't gonna happen."

"You met the girl once and you know that . . . how?"

Sam Starr realized he'd made a mistake. Now he had to do something to get Belle's mind off of it.

"You know," he said, running his big hand down over her flat belly until it was buried in her crotch, "I think we should stop talkin' about her and pay some more attention to us."

He slid as finger into her wet pussy and Belle bit her lips and made a hissing sound.

"Well," she said, reaching for his cock and holding it tightly, "I think you got a point, there!"

***

The saloon remained empty while she struggled with her thought over her beer. In the end she decided to stick with her original course. Head for Missouri, catch up to Jed Harlow, and make him tell the truth. For that she needed a horse.

She stood up, went back to the bar with the empty mug, and asked the bartender, "You know anybody with a horse for sale?"

"Sorry," he said, shaking his head, "that's not my business. You could check at the livery stable, though."

"Yeah, thanks," she said, "and thanks for the beer."

"Any time," he said. "You brought a little bit of life into my day. I thank you for that."

She waved and went out the doors.

***

Belle got dressed while Sam watched.

"Come on," she said, "move yer sweet ass out."

"What's there to do?" he asked. "We might as well wait here for the rest of 'em to get to town." He didn't want to run into Roxy, again.

"I wanna find Roxy," Belle said. "Make my offer."

"Not me," he said. "I'm gonna take a nap. You wore me out, woman."

"You know, Sam," she said, "it's lucky you're so damned pretty." She strapped on her gun. "I'll be back later."

"I'll be here," he said, rolling over.

As she left, he fervently hoped that Roxy Doyle's horse had recovered, and she had left town.

***

Roxy figured not enough time had gone by for the vet to treat her roan, or to find her another horse. She needed to ask somebody else about it. Maybe another bartender in a different saloon, or perhaps there was another livery.

She was walking down Coffeyville's Eighth street when she heard, "Roxy, hey Roxy!"

She turned and saw Belle Starr running across the street toward her. She was glad to see that Sam wasn't with her.

"I was lookin' for you," Belle said.

"I thought you were with Sam."

Belle grinned broadly.

"I wore the poor man out," she said. "He's takin' a nap. What're you up to?"

"I checked with the vet on my horse. He says he's going to need days to heal, maybe a week. So I've got to look for somebody with a horse to trade, or sell . . . cheap."

"Why don't we go someplace and talk?" Belle said.

"I really need to find a horse."

"I know people in this town," Belle said. "I can get you a horse."

"That's great!"

"But first, I want you to hear my offer," Belle said. "I tell you what. I'll pay you to listen."

"Pay me?"

Belle nodded.

"Fifty dollars, just to come with me to a saloon and have a drink."

"Fifty?"

"Enough to buy you a horse."

Roxy thought that with fifty dollars and her horse to trade, she might even get a decent one.

"A drink?"

"One drink," Belle said. "Come on, Roxy. Whataya say?"

"I say," Roxy replied, "which saloon?"

Chapter Thirty-Four

Belle picked out the saloon, one on the other side of town from the small one Roxy had just come from. There other patrons in the place, who were at once attracted by Roxy and repelled by Belle Starr. Roxy could feel them shrink away as she and Belle approached the bar.

"Two beers, Vin," Belle said to the tall, gangly and decidedly dirty looking bartender.

"Sure thing, Belle."

When Belle had both beers in her hands she said to Vin, "Make sure nobody bothers us."

Vin smiled nervously and asked, "Who would bother you, Belle?"

"Come on," she said, and led Roxy to a table in the rear. Men at nearby tables got up and found seats further away.

"They're all afraid of you," Roxy observed.

"It's man's world, Roxy," Belle said. "If we wanna get by, we have to make men afraid of us. Believe me, they're afraid of you, too."

"They don't even know who I am."

"I'm sure they do," Belle said. "You stand out. I knew who you were right away. But even if they don't, they recognize you for what you are."

"And what's that?" Roxy asked.

"Dangerous," Belle said. "You and me, we're dangerous, and men know that."

Roxy wasn't sure if she liked being put in the same class as Belle Starr. After all, Belle was an outlaw, and Roxy usually stayed on the right side of the law.

"What's this offer you've got for me, Belle?" Roxy asked. "And, oh, there's the little matter of fifty dollars."

"I like that," Belle said. "You're a good businesswoman, too." Belle reached into her pocket, took out some paper money, counted out fifty dollars and passed it across the table to Roxy, who tucked it away in her shirt pocket.

"Okay, then." Roxy sipped her beer, and waited.

"It goes like this," Belle said. "Sam and me, we're waitin' here for the rest of our gang to show up. We got a job to pull, a big one, and we could use another hand—a hand like you."

"What's the job?" Roxy asked.

"I'll tell you when the time comes," Belle said. "First I wanna hear if you're interested."

"How much would I stand to make?" Roxy asked, to keep Belle talking.

"At least five thousand a piece," Belle said.

"And who else is involved?"

"Like I said, the rest of the Starr gang. There's Wee Willie Garrett, Teddy Jellicoe, Alfredo Juarez—"

"I don't know any of those names," Roxy said.

"They're good men," Belle said, "and it suits me that they're not well known."

"What are you going to want me to do?"

"Back my play, whatever it is."

"I won't go in for torture, Belle," Roxy said. "That's not my style."

Belle's face clouded. There was a story that in 1873 she and her then husband, Jim Reed, tortured a husband and wife until they revealed the whereabouts of $30,000 in gold coins they had hidden in the Indian territories.

"That's an old wives' tale," Belle told Roxy. "I ain't never tortured nobody, and neither has Sam. I've killed people, yeah, but they got in the way of me and what I wanted. I regard myself as a woman who has seen much of life. And I don't snuff it out for just no reason."

"I don't know that I want to kill anybody, either. Not even for five thousand dollars."

"Look," Belle said, "I ain't gonna ask you to do anythin' you don't wanna do. And you might be interested in meetin' somebody else who might be comin' along."

"Who's that?"

Belle grinned. "Jesse James."

"Jesse James?" Roxy was surprised. "I thought he was retired."

"Since we're near Missouri," Belle said, "I thought I'd use this job to lure him outta retirement."

"What about Frank?"

"Frank ain't in Missouri," Belle said. "Fact is, I don't know where Frank is. But Jesse's livin' there with Zee, under the name Tom Howard."

Roxy had to admit she wouldn't have minded meeting Jesse James. From the stories she'd heard, she'd formed an opinion that he wasn't the blood thirsty outlaw people claimed he was. She also knew that he was acquainted with Clint Adams, and the Gunsmith didn't usually make friends with killers.

"I thought that'd get your attention," Belle said. "You wanna think about this for a while?"

"I do," Roxy said. "And I can think it over while I'm looking for a new horse."

"That's fine," Belle said. "You'll be needin' a horse."

They finished their beers and stood up to leave. Patrons around them tensed, thinking perhaps the two women were about to draw down on each other.

"Idiots," Belle said. "Come on, let's get out of here."

Outside Roxy asked, "What's the rest of your day going to be like?"

"I'm gonna go back to the hotel, wake up my beautiful Cherokee husband and fuck his brains out some more," Belle said, with a smile. "Why don't you find a man and do the same thing?"

"I might do that," Roxy lied, "but after I've gotten myself a horse."

"There's a spread just North of town, owned by a fella named Jellicoe."

"Your gang member?"

"His family," Belle admitted. "But they got horses, might have one for sale. Rent yourself a buggy and take a ride out there."

"I'll do that, Belle," Roxy said. "Thanks."

The two ladies went their separate ways.

Chapter Thirty-Five

Roxy decided to do just what Belle suggested—not the finding a man part, but riding out to the Jellicoe ranch to look at some horses. To rent a buggy she went back to Dandy's livery stable to see what the vet had.

"Still working on him," Dandy said, as Roxy entered.

"I know you are," she said, "I'm not checking on that. You got a horse and buggy I can rent?"

"Sure," Dandy said. "It's not a good horse, but it'll get you where you're goin'—dependin' on where you're goin'."

"The Jellicoe place."

Dandy frowned. "What you goin' out there, for?"

"Belle Starr said they might sell me a horse."

"Well," Dandy said, "I wouldn't normally recommend that anybody go out there, but if you can drop Belle's name, that might make a difference."

"Rough place?" she asked.

"The roughest," Dandy said. "There's usually one or two outlaws hidin' out there—and Jellicoe's son is in Belle's gang."

"Yeah, she told me that."

"Seems like you and Belle are gettin' close," Dandy said.

"I wouldn't say that, exactly," Roxy said, "but we've got some things in common."

"I bet you do," Dandy said. "Come on, the buggy's out back, and the horse is in the corral. I'll hitch it up for you."

***

Roxy watched as Dandy hitched the tired looking mare up to the buggy. If she was looking to take Belle's advice about a man she could have done worse than the vet, Dandy, but she didn't want to form that kind of a relationship with him. Better to keep this businesslike.

"There you go," he said, backing away from the rig. "Like I said, she's kinda old and slow, but she'll get you there and back."

"I'm much obliged, Dandy," Roxy said. "How much do I owe you?"

"Save your money to buy that horse," he said. "Let's just call this a loan."

"I appreciate it. Tell me, can I trade the roan as part of a deal for a new horse?"

"I don't see why not," he said. "Once the leg heals, he'll be fine."

"Good," she said, "Do you know this Jellicoe personally?"

"Yeah, I've been out there a time or two for a sick horse or cow."

"You get along?"

"We get along because they need me," Dandy said. "They get along with people they need. Other than that, they don't want nobody out there."

"Well," she said, "I guess this is going to be interesting, then."

***

Roxy followed Dandy's directions to the Jellicoe ranch. She spotted the spread from a distance, and when she reached it she saw a working ranch with a worn but solid house, bunkhouse, barn and corral. As she rode up to the main house men stopped the work they were doing to watch her.

When she reached the house she reined the horse in, but remained in the seat of the buggy, waiting for somebody to approach her.

A group of ranch hands drifted over, following one man in particular.

"Can we help you?" the man asked. He was a rough-hewn man who looked as if he had been chipped out of granite. He was probably in his late forties, but was carrying it very well.

"I'm looking for the man in charge," she said.

"That'd be me," he said. "The name's Jellicoe. I own this place. Who are you?"

"My name's Roxy Doyle," she said.

"You're takin' a big chance, Miss Doyle, ridin' out here alone. Some of these men ain't never seen a woman looks like you."

"Well. I have a friend who said I could ride out here and be treated properly.

"Is that right?" Jellicoe asked. "And just who would that be?"

"Belle Starr."

Jellicoe frowned at her, obviously trying to decide if she was telling the truth.

"You know Belle?"

She nodded

"And Sam."

"Yeah," he said, "I'll bet you know Sam." He folded his arms. The men behind him were still eyeing her. "Why would Belle send you out here? You wanted?"

"Not that I know of," Roxy said. "I'm looking for a horse. Mine injured his leg when I got to town."

"So? It'll heal."

"I need a horse before that," Roxy said. "Belle's got something she wants me to do."

Jellicoe was conflicted.

"Look," Roxy said, "your men don't seem to be doing much other than ogling me. Why not send one of them to town to ask Belle if she knows me?"

Suddenly, the men behind him were all backing away. Obviously, nobody wanted to talk to Belle Starr, and they were all thinking of something else they could be doing.

Jellicoe turned and said, "Relax, nobody's goin' to town. But you all better get back to work!"

The men all started to scatter, some walking, some running. Jellicoe turned back to face Roxy.

"What about it?" Roxy asked.

"Step on down from there," Jellicoe said, "and we'll see what we can do."

Chapter Thirty-Six

Jellicoe had someone take care of Roxy's horse and buggy, then took her to the barn, where he had a full office, with a large desk and a file cabinet. She wondered, if the Jellicoe ranch was a haven for outlaws how come, Jellicoe needed a file cabinet?

"Let's have a drink first," he said, grabbing a bottle from a small table in the corner. "Whiskey?"

"Sure, why not?"

He poured two glasses and handed her one. "I get who you are now."

"Do you?"

"You're the girl they call Lady Gunsmith," he said.

"That's right," she said, "Roxy Doyle."

"You're also Gavin Doyle's kid."

Roxy stopped with the glass halfway to her mouth.

"So you *knew* my father?"

"I *know* your father," Jellicoe corrected.

"So you're not one of those people who thinks he's dead…?"

Jellicoe didn't say anything.

"I asked you a question."

Jellicoe hesitated, then said. "Let's just say I'll believe it when I see it."

"That's how I feel." She drank some whiskey. "Do you know a man named Harlow?"

"Jed Harlow? Sure. He's been here once or twice to hide out." Jellicoe drank his whiskey down, then poured himself another. He held the bottle up to Roxy, who shook her head.

"You got any idea where he might be now?" she asked.

"I'm in the habit of hidin' people who are runnin' from the law," he said.

"I'm *not* the law."

"Then why are you askin' about him?"

"I heard he was in Missouri," she said. "I'm looking for him."

"Like I said, why?"

"I saw him in Kingman, Arizona a while back. He gave me a bum steer that sent me to Ellsworth, Kansas. Said my father had been killed in a card game. Turned out to be a lie."

"So, you wanna ask him again?"

"I do."

He sat in his desk chair and leaned back.

"You're a helluva good-lookin' woman."

"What's that got to do with anything?"

Jellicoe shrugged. "There ain't so many women like you come through here."

"What about Belle?"

He laughed. "She may be as dangerous as you, but she ain't as good-lookin', that's for sure."

"Don't you have a wife?"

"Like I said," Jellicoe went on, "not so many good-lookin' women here."

Roxy sighed. "What do you want?"

"I want a good look at you," he said. "At what you've got."

"And then you'll tell me about Harlow?"

"You heard he was in Missouri."

"That's right."

"You show me your sweet wares, and I'll tell you exactly where he's at."

She took off her hat, tossed it aside and shook out her beautiful red hair. Then she pulled her shirt out of her jeans, unbuttoned it, and peeled it off. Naked to the waist she put her hands on her hips and let Jellicoe have a look.

Jellicoe stared at her with his mouth open, his eyes glazed. Ten years after her first experience she still didn't quite understand this part. What was so unusual about a pair of tits?

"Jesus H. Christ!" Jellicoe said.

"Happy?" she asked.

He stood up from his chair, and she could see the huge bulge in his pants.

"I wanna touch 'em," he said.

"Well," she said, "come around and touch them."

He stumbled in his attempt to get around the desk so fast. As he came toward her with his hands out, she hurriedly backed away so that his hands closed on air.

"I think," she said, "I'd like to see *your* wares."

"What?"

"Show me what's in your pants," she said.

She didn't have to ask him twice. He wasn't wearing a gun, so he unbuckled his pants, dropped them to his ankles, followed by his dirty drawers. His erection was huge, thick, and ugly as sin.

Hiding her distaste, Roxy reached out with one hand and took hold of it.

"Oh, God!" he said, as she stroked it lightly.

"Now," she said, "before we go any further, where will I find Jed Harlow?"

"I-if you just sit tight," he said, "he'll be comin' here with Jesse James. They're both comin' to join Belle and her gang."

Roxy frowned. Belle hadn't mentioned that. But then, had she told Belle she was looking for Jed Harlow? She couldn't remember.

"Well, thank you very much, Mr. Jellicoe," she said, releasing his penis. "Now can we get to the horse trading?"

He licked his lips. "First get them pants off, gal! You wanna know what this thing feels like inside ya, don't ya?"

"Actually," Roxy said, "I don't."

"Wha—"

"Not interested, Jellicoe. All I want from you is a horse."

Jellicoe stared at her big, rust colored nipples and seemed about to cry.

"You bitch!" he said, growing angry. But as he reached for her, she drew her gun and pressed the barrel to his crotch.

"What the hell—"

"First," she said, "I'll open your office door so your men can see you with your pants down, and then I'll shoot your pecker off."

"Wha—you can't—"

"Or we can go out and look at some horses. What do you say?"

Now he didn't know whether to be angry, sad, or scared.

"Okay, okay," he said. "Lemme pull my pants up, damn it!"

She took the gun away from his dick, holstered it and backed away. While he cinched his belt, she grabbed her shirt and put it back on.

When they were both decent he growled, "I got horses back in the corral. Come on."

Chapter Thirty-Seven

Roxy made the trip back to town with a new horse tied to the rear of the buggy. But now that she knew Jed Harlow would be coming to Coffeyville to meet up with Belle Starr, there was really no reason for her to leave town. What she needed to do now was convince Belle that she was interested in her proposal, when she truly wasn't. She had no desire to rob a train or bank or stagecoach with the Belle Starr gang. All she wanted was to face Harlow again, and make him tell the truth.

And maybe meet Jesse James.

She took the horse and buggy back to Dandy's livery, where the man was still working. He paused as she drove it inside.

"Back in one piece, I see," he said.

"Not without some effort."

"What's that mean?"

"Let's just say Mr. Jellicoe and I came to an understanding," she said, stepping down.

"You must have," Dandy said, walking around to the rear of the buggy. "That's a fine looking gelding. What's he, five or six?"

"Six," she said. "Can you give him a once over for me, make sure he's as sound as I think he is."

"What about the roan?" he asked.

"It's Jellicoe's," she said. "When he heals you can deliver him out there."

"And how much did this one cost you?"

"Just the roan."

Dandy looked surprised. "Just a straight up swap? You and Jellicoe must have come to some real good understandin'."

She just smiled.

"Well, I guess I'll look him over and have him ready so you can leave—"

"Oh, I'm not leaving," she said. "I've decided Belle's offer is too interesting to pass up."

"It doesn't seem to me you'd give a proposal from Belle much serious consideration."

"Well, you never know, do you?" she asked.

"Have you told her that, yet?"

"No, not yet," Roxy said. "I'm going to find her now and tell her."

"So you'll be in town at least a few days more, then?"

"Looks like."

"Maybe we can have supper one night," he said, "get to know each other a little better."

"Yeah," she said, poking him in the chest with her forefinger, "maybe."

But that was all she gave him, and left.

***

She went to the Onion to see if Belle and Sam were in their room, but there was no answer when she knocked on the door, and no sounds from inside.

She went down to the lobby and approached the desk clerk.

"You seen Belle and Sam Starr anywhere?"

"They came down a little while ago," he said, with a grin. "Looked pretty tired, if ya know what I mean."

"Never mind that," she said. "Where'd they go?"

"I heard them say they were gonna get somethin' to eat, but they didn't go into our dining room, so I don't know where they went."

"Anybody else check in while I was away?"

"If you mean did any other members of their gang show up yet, no."

She wondered, did everybody in town know that Belle was waiting for her gang?

"Thanks," she said, and left the hotel.

Out on the boardwalk she looked both ways, and across the street. There were plenty of cafes and restaurants in the growing town. She could either spend time looking in windows and trying to find them, or wait for them to come and find her. She decided on the former, and the easiest way for that to happen was for her to be in a saloon, one that was doing a decent business.

She decided on The Red Slipper Saloon, which she'd passed several times but never gone into. It always seemed busy enough, and would serve her purpose.

***

The Red Slipper was, indeed, a busy saloon and gambling hall. Roxy could hear the music and loud voices of many patrons as she approached the front. There was a sign over the door, no name, just a painting of a red slipper.

As she entered she thought she'd like it there. It was so crowded she'd be able to blend in, drawing less stares than usual. But as she approached the bar she did see a man or two nudge his compadre and jerk a chin or thumb her way. Maybe Clint Adams was right years ago when he suggested she might cut her hair and wear ill fitting clothes.

She managed to elbow herself some room at the bar and order a beer. The busy bartender brought it, took a quick look at her, but didn't have time to stare, as he had many other customers.

Clint Adams had also told her there'd be no end to the saloons she'd be seeing if she continued her search for her father. She took it a step further. Even if she stopped searching, she'd still be drifting, and there'd always be another town, another hotel and another saloon. That was, of course, if she didn't settle down somewhere, which didn't seem likely. Her experience with living in a house with other people had not been a good one. Of course, she could settle down and live alone, but it would take money to buy a place. She'd taken jobs to make money, but that was only to fill her pockets to get to the next town.

Of course, the five thousand dollars that Belle was promising her could change all that.

Maybe it *was* time to give Belle's proposal some serious consideration.

Chapter Thirty-Eight

Roxy had to brush off several indecent proposals from drunken cowboys before Belle and Sam Starr came into the Red Slipper.

The Starrs attracted a lot of attention when they walked in, because everybody in Coffeyville knew who they were. They drank it in, then looked around, saw Roxy and started over to her. Belle approached with a big smile on her face, while Sam walked behind her, looking worried.

"Roxy!" Belle Starr threw her arms around her and hugged her tightly.

Roxy didn't like the hug, it pinned her gun hand to her side, so she untangled herself from it as soon as possible, without offending Belle.

"Why don't you let me buy you two a beer?" Roxy said, waving at the bartender.

"Sure thing, sweetie," Belle said. "Come on, Sam. Make us some room."

But Sam didn't need to make room. The men nearby had already moved to either side, making sure the Starrs could get to the bar.

The bartender set three fresh cold beers out for Roxy, Belle and Sam.

"So," Belle said, after a healthy sip, "did you go out and see Jellicoe?"

"I did," Roxy said, "and I came back with a horse."

"He must have made you a rough deal," Sam said. "Jellicoe's known for that."

"Actually," Roxy said, "we came to a straight up trade agreement."

"A straight trade for your injured horse?" Belle asked. "What did you do to him?"

Roxy smiled. "We came to an understanding."

Belle laughed, and looked at Sam. "I told you she was dangerous, didn't I?"

"She traded for a horse, Belle," Sam said. "Don't overreact."

"The only way Jellicoe would've traded straight up for a wounded horse," Belle said, "was if Lady Gunsmith made him do it."

Sam looked at Roxy, and she smiled. She felt bad for him, but he was still a man who wasn't giving her enough credit.

"What's the matter, Sam?" she asked. "Did you think I couldn't get what I wanted from a man like Jellicoe?"

"I guess I was wrong," he said.

"You bet you were," Belle said, putting her arm around Roxy's shoulders. "She can get anythin' she wants from any man."

Belle turned Roxy to the bar, but Roxy was able to give Sam a look over her shoulder. Sam just shook his head, and took up position next to Belle, his hand around his beer.

"Now that you have a horse, have you thought some more about my offer?" Belle asked.

"Actually, I have," Roxy said, trying to sound enthusiastic. "I'm thinking it sounds really interesting."

"I thought you might."

Roxy leaned over and lowered her voice. "Especially the Jesse James part."

Belle held her forefinger to her lips.

"Let's keep that to ourselves," she said.

"Well, I was wondering," Roxy said, lowering her voice, "Jellicoe said something about some others coming with Jesse."

"Did he?"

"Yes, he did," Roxy said, "and I was wondering who they might be."

"I think," Belle said, "if Jesse's bringin' somebody else along, we'll just have to wait to see who it is. But knowin' Jesse like I do, I'd say it's gonna be somebody who can pull his weight."

Roxy decided she'd better stop pressing, for now.

"Good point," she said. "Is there anything else I'm going to need?"

"Just your gun," Belle said, "and a good horse."

"Well, I've got the gun," Roxy said, "and Dandy is checking the horse for me to make sure he's as sound as I think he is."

"Then we're set," Belle said. "We're just waitin' for the rest of the boys, and Jesse."

Roxy looked over at Sam, whose eyes were roaming over the crowded room. Roxy thought he might just be checking for trouble, but then noticed that he was watching the saloon girls in their pretty dresses. Suddenly she realized, a smart woman like Belle would have to know what kind of man she was married to, so it probably wouldn't surprise her to discover that Sam had slept with Roxy. But, she wondered, who would Belle hold that against, her or her husband?

She didn't want to find out.

***

Later on Belle decided she wanted a table, and sent Sam to find one. Since they were all taken, Roxy watched Sam walk over to a table of three men, speak to them amiably, pointing over to Roxy and Belle. When he was done, all three men simply rose and walked out the door. Sam then waved to the two ladies.

"What did you say to them?" Roxy asked, curiously.

"Just that Belle Starr and Lady Gunsmith were tired of standing, wanted a table and decided to get this one."

"You didn't threaten them did you?"

"I didn't have to," Sam said.

"Sam, honey, would you get us three more beers?" Belle asked.

"Sure, Belle."

As he went to the bar Roxy said, "One of these girls would have gotten drinks for us."

"I know," she said, "but Sam needs to be kept in line from time to time. Also, I didn't want one of those pretty girls comin' over here and flirtin' with him."

"You think they would have?" Roxy asked. "Right in front of you?"

"Yep," Belle said, "because Sam is that pretty, and then if one of them had flirted with him, I might've shot her dead."

"Just for flirting?" Roxy asked.

Belle looked Roxy right in the eye and said, "Just for flirting."

Chapter Thirty-Nine

While they continued to drink, Sam Starr looked worried, Roxy listened and Belle Starr did most of the talking.

When the batwings swung inward and a Mexican stepped through, Belle stopped talking. He was not tall, maybe 5'8", rather thickly built, with twin bandoliers of shells crisscrossing his chest.

"There's Alfredo," she said. "Run over and get him, Sam."

Sam got up, but he didn't run. Still, he went over and got Alfredo Juarez's attention, then brought him back to the table.

"So happy to see you, Senora Belle," he said.

"Alfredo, this is Roxy Doyle. You may know her as—"

"—Lady Gunsmith," Juarez said. "A pleasure, Senorita."

Juarez was not handsome, and had several silver teeth, but his mannerisms were gentlemanly, and charming.

"The pleasure is mine, Alfredo," Roxy said.

"Get yourself a beer and then come back here and sit," Belle told him. "We're still waitin' on the others."

He smiled warmly at Roxy and said, "I shall return."

As the Mexican went for a beer, Belle said to Roxy, "Watch out for that one. He don't look like much, but he'll charm the pants off ya."

"I'll keep that in mind."

Alfredo returned with a beer, sat between Belle and Roxy, and said, "I just rode in. Did not even have time to get a hotel room. I need this." He lifted his beer and drank half of it down.

"You've got a room at the Onion," Belle said, "but you'll have to bunk with Teddy Jellicoe."

"Why does he need a room, when his father lives right outside of town?" Juarez asked.

"Just until everybody gets here."

"Well, if I must, I must," Juarez said. He looked at Roxy. "I do not like him, but I can keep from killing him for one night."

"That sounds wise," Roxy said.

"And will Senorita Roxy be joining us?" he asked.

"You bet she is," Belle said. "We can use her gun, *and* her smarts."

"Ah," Juarez said, "smart, good with a gun, and beautiful. All of the legend is true, then."

"I don't know about that," Roxy said, "but thank you."

"I must toast two such smart women," Juarez said, holding up his half full beer mug.

"I'll drink to that," Sam said, raising his glass.

"We all will," Belle said, and she and Roxy raised their glasses before they all drank.

"And now I will go to my room and get rid of some of this dust," Juarez said. He stood and bowed to both women. "*Con permiso*?"

"You go ahead, 'fredo," Belle said. "We'll be right here."

"Senora, Senorita." He looked at Sam. "Amigo."

As Juarez went out the door Roxy asked, "When are the others due?"

"Probably tomorrow," Belle said. "And Jesse—well, Jesse's on his own time. He'll get here when he gets here."

"With whoever he's bringing with him, right?" Roxy asked.

"Right."

"I think I'm gonna find a poker game," Sam said, looking around.

"In here?" Belle asked.

"Naw, I think I'll go over to Pat Gulicks's place." He stood up. "I'll see you at the hotel, Belle."

"Not too late, darlin'. I still got plans for you."

He tipped his hat to Roxy and left.

"You make him nervous," Belle said.

"Do I? Why?" Roxy asked, innocently.

"You're so beautiful he don't know where to look," Belle said. "And he thinks I'll get mad."

"And you won't?"

"Why should I?" Belle asked. "I'm the one who invited you, and you ain't playin' up to him, at all."

"I wouldn't," Roxy said. "He's your husband, and I know that."

"And he knows it to," she said. "He knows if I caught him with another woman, I'd cut it off."

"So you've never caught him?" Roxy asked.

"Never," Belle said. "Mind you, that don't mean he ain't cheated on me. Women are always throwing themselves at my Sam. But as long as I don't get wind of it, or I don't catch him, he's safe."

Roxy finished her fourth? fifth? Beer and set the empty mug down.

"I've had enough," she said. "I'm going back to my room."

"Aw, you gonna leave me here alone?" Belle asked.

"If I fall asleep at this table, it'll still be like you're alone," Roxy told her. "I've had a full day."

"Okay, go ahead," she said. "I'll find somebody here who's got the balls to have a drink with me. Or maybe one of my boys might show up. 'fredo will probably come back. You go ahead and turn in."

"I'll see you tomorrow," Roxy said.

"Breakfast in the hotel," Belle said.

"Okay."

Belle was squinting across the room as Roxy left, looking for somebody she wouldn't mind having a drink with.

With all that talk about what she'd do if she caught Sam cheating on her, Roxy walked back to the Onion wondering if Belle had ever cheated on Sam. She seemed to have a pretty good appetite for sex.

When the shot rang out Roxy reacted immediately. She hit the ground rolling as the second shot sounded, came up on one knee with her gun in her hand.

It was dark, and she was waiting for the muzzle flash of a third shot to show her where the shooter was, but it never came.

A crowd came charging out of the Red Slipper, led by Belle Starr.

"What the hell—" she said, reaching Roxy, holding her gun. "Somebody shootin' at you?"

"Looks like it."

"You see where it came from?" Belle asked.

"Nope," Roxy said, "I was too busy rolling on the ground, trying not to get shot."

Alfredo Juarez came running over and Belle shouted at him, "Get across the street and see what you can find!"

"Si!" he replied, and disappeared into the dark.

Next, Sheriff Marks came running over. "What the hell happened?"

"Somebody took two shots at Roxy," Belle said. "Where were you?"

"Doin' my rounds," Marks said. He looked at Roxy. "You okay?"

"I'm fine." She holstered her gun. "I'm sure they're gone."

"Where'd the shot come from?"

"I'm guessing across the street," Roxy said. "I never saw anything."

"I'll take a look."

"I sent one of my men," Belle said. "If there's anythin' there, he'll find it."

"Who?"

"Juarez."

"That Mex?"

"He's a good man."

"I'll take a look, anyway," Marks said. To Roxy: "Where you gonna be?"

"I was headed for my hotel," she said. "That's where I'll be."

"Don't you want a drink?" Belle asked.

"I've been shot at before, Belle," Roxy assured her.

"Everybody off the street!" Marks shouted. "It's all over."

As people filed back into the saloon, Marks headed across to see what he could find.

"You want me to walk you to the hotel, in case they try again?" Belle asked.

"It's just down the street, Belle. And I think they're gone. I'll be fine."

Belle smiled. "I knew I picked the right girl for this job!"

"I'll see you in the morning," Roxy said, and started for the Onion again.

Chapter Forty

Roxy entered her room and hung her gunbelt on the bedpost. She sat and removed her boots. She avoided the window, just in case, and took the one straight-backed wooden chair in the room, jamming it beneath the doorknob. Then she sat on the bed.

What she told Belle was true, she had been shot at before, but that didn't mean she liked it, or was used to it. And the only reason she could figure it happened here in Coffeyville was that damn name, Lady Gunsmith. Somebody obviously wanted to claim they killed her, and didn't mind doing it from behind, in the dark.

What other reason could there be?

Sam Starr, so she wouldn't tell Belle she'd slept with him?

Somebody from Belle's gang, who didn't want her involved in their next job? And, if so, who was in town besides Alfredo Juarez?

Could the rancher, Jellicoe, have sent someone—maybe his son? —to kill her because she had humiliated him?

And what about Belle? She seemed very concerned when she came running out, but had she put someone up to it, afraid that Sam was attracted to Roxy?

Or did she actually know that they had slept together. Had Sam slipped? Or had someone else told her? And if so, who? Who else knew?

Roxy scolded herself. She was going to have to be more careful in the future. Men were too quick to lie.

She decided not to suspect Belle. The Outlaw Queen's liking for her seemed to be genuine or, at least, her desire to have Roxy be part of her gang, for this new job.

She decided to just go to sleep, making sure first that her gun would slide easily out of the holster, should someone try to come busting through her door. At least she was confident there was no access from outside the window, and she doubted that anyone would take the chance of being seen setting a ladder against the wall. Clint Adams had taught her to be careful, but not to let her imagination run away with itself.

***

In the morning she found Belle Starr waiting for her at a table in the dining room.

"No Sam this morning?" she asked, sitting.

"I wore the sweet man out again last night," Belle said. "He'll be down later. It's just you and me, this mornin'."

"What about Juarez?"

"He can get his own breakfast," Belle said. "Besides, I think he spent the night in a whorehouse. He's a good man in a fight, but not somebody I want to eat with."

"I've known those kinds of men, myself," Roxy said.

"You talk real educated," Belle said. "Where you from?"

"Came from the East with my parents," Roxy said. "After my Ma was killed by Indians and my Pa went off to become a bounty hunter, I was raised by a Mormon couple.

That didn't go so well, so I left when I was fifteen. Been on my own ever since. I had some schooling back East, and in Utah Territory. Since then I've educated myself along the way. I don't want to talk to people and sound ignorant—no offense," she added, quickly. "I'm not saying you're ignorant—"

"Hell, none taken," Belle said. "Fact is, I had a formal education in Missouri at an institution my father founded. I've done the opposite of you. My speech pattern has changed over the years to match the people I work or live with. Sam's Cherokee, no education to speak of. I know I sound hard and rough sometimes, but I aim to. Men have got to know the deal with me on even terms."

"I think you get that message across," Roxy said.

"So have you," Belle said, "and it ain't been easy, right?"

"You're right about that," Roxy said, "and it still ain't getting any easier."

They ordered breakfast and talked some more over coffee while waiting for it. At one point, Sheriff Marks came into the room and walked over to their table.

"'mornin', Sheriff," Belle said. "What can we do for you?"

"I want you to know Teddy Jellicoe just rode in, and he's got Wee Willie with him."

"Well, that's good news," Belle said.

"For you, maybe," Marks said, "but I remember the last time they were here. I can't have them shootin' up the town again, Belle."

"Relax, Sheriff," Belle said, "nobody's gonna shoot up your town."

"Oh no? What about last night?"

"That wasn't our fault," Belle said. "Somebody musta recognized Roxy and decided to make a play for her. You find anything across the street?"

"Nothin'."

"Neither did Alfredo," Belle said

"It doesn't matter," Roxy said. "What's done is done. We can't let it distract us."

"You got that right." She looked at Marks. "When I finish my breakfast I'll make sure Willie and Teddy get the message, Sheriff."

"How much longer you intend to be in Coffeyville, Belle?" he asked.

"A day or two, no more," Belle said. "We're still waitin' for a coupla men. Why, you sayin' you wanna run me outta town?"

"No, no Belle," Marks said, "I ain't sayin' that at all. You know you and Sam are always welcome here."

"I do know that, Sheriff," Belle said, "that's why I'm gonna have my men on their best behavior." The waiter came with their food. "Now Roxy and me, we wanna eat our breakfast in peace."

"Sure, Belle, sure," Marks said. "I'll, uh, be goin'."

"Don't worry so much," Belle said. "Everythin's gonna be just fine."

Marks withdrew, taking his worried look with him. The two women started to eat.

Chapter Forty-One

After breakfast Roxy and Belle went outside, stood in front of the hotel.

"I gotta go find those two idiots," Belle said.

"Jellicoe and Wee Willie?'

Belle nodded. "If I don't get to them, they'll shoot up the town. We don't need the attention."

"Especially not after last night," Roxy said.

"That wasn't your fault," Belle said. "If I find out who took those shots at you, I'll take care of them myself."

"I don't think we will find out, Belle," Roxy said. "It was just somebody looking to make a name for themselves, even if it was for backshooting Lady Gunsmith."

"You can let that go?"

"Believe me," Roxy said, "I don't know who's taken half the shots at me in my life. Don't worry about it."

"Well," Belle said, "I can't say I ain't been shot at my-self."

"I guess I'll go over to the livery and check on that new horse," Roxy said.

"Good idea," Belle agreed. "Let's meet up in front of the Onion in a couple of hours. By then I'll know who's in town, and who we're waitin' for."

"Okay," Roxy said, "I'll see you then."

They went their separate ways, Belle to find her men and Roxy to talk with Dandy about the new horse.

***

When she got to the livery she didn't find Dandy there. The two horses—the roan and new gelding—were in stalls, standing quietly. She was about to call out Dandy's name when she heard some noise coming from the back. She went to investigate.

She came to a wooden door, determined that the sounds she was hearing were coming from inside, but now she thought she knew what they were. She pushed the door open a crack and saw that she was right. She'd been hearing water, and there was Dandy, in a big, wooden bathtub, as naked as the day he was born. She watched with interest as he cleaned himself with soap and a washcloth. She couldn't remember ever having spied on a man who was bathing, before. He washed his hair, the back of his neck, his face, under his arms. Then he started washing things she couldn't see, rubbing them real good. He let his head drop back and she could see that his right arm was still moving. Finally, he brought his head forward, braced his hands on the side of the tub and stood up. Water sluiced down over his naked body. He was standing with his back to her, using the washcloth to clean his butt. She watched this with great interest, because he was tall, rangy, and had a good body—especially his butt.

She decided to surprise him.

She pushed the door open and walked in. "Dandy, I didn't see you out front—oops. Sorry."

He turned quickly, looking surprised, then when he saw her he relaxed.

"Oh, that's okay," he said. "I'm almost done."

"You're in pretty good shape for a vet," she said.

"It's all those big animals I have to wrangle around," he said, still looking at her over his shoulder. "If you give me a minute I'll dry off and come on out."

"Oh, that's okay," she said, leaning against the wall. "Don't mind me. I'm enjoying the view. That is, unless you're too shy."

To answer that question he turned around to face her. His cock was almost fully hard, and was now pointing at her. It was long and had what she could only describe as a kind of graceful arc to it. It looked like it would fit right in—

"I'm getting' out," he warned her.

"Go ahead."

He stepped out of the tub, continued to face her and dried off. As he wiped his torso, his hard prick bobbed about.

"I think you're going to have some trouble getting that into your pants," she commented.

"I think you're right," he said, "and you being here ain't exactly helping matters."

"That right?" she asked pushing away from the wall. "Then maybe I can help."

She approached, stopped in front of him and took the towel from his hand. Then she looked down at his cock, fully hard now, and started to dry it for him.

"Here," she said, moving the towel down, "I'll get these for you, too."

As she rubbed his balls with the towel he made a sort of growling noise and grabbed her by the shoulders. She looked into his face just in time for him to pull her close and kiss her.

As they kissed, Roxy dropped the towel so she could take his penis in one hand, and slide the other around to cup one of his ass cheeks.

"One of us has too many clothes on," he said, breathless, after they broke the kiss.

"That would be me," she said, "but we can solve that problem."

She stepped back, first removed the gunbelt and set it nearby, then her clothes. When she was totally naked, except for her boots she looked at him, at the naked lust that had taken over his face.

"Boots on or off?" she asked.

"On!" he said. "I can't wait any longer."

He closed in on her, gathered her into his arms and lifted her off her feet. He carried her over to a couple of bales of hay against one wall and set her down on them. Then he began to kiss and lick her big breasts, biting down on the nipples, just hard enough. It seemed he was a man who had some idea of what he was doing when he was with a woman. This was not going to be a grunt-and-spurt session.

She turned so that her legs were dangling over the sides, giving him access to crouch between her thighs and bury his face. She rested her calves on his shoulders and settled with her back against the wall to enjoy while he made a meal of her.

She stood it for as long as she possibly could, and when it felt too good to be true, she gently pushed him away.

"You're making me crazy." She sat up and reached for him. "Come here." Pulling him close she grabbed his cock, ran her hand up and down it lightly. "Some curve, I've never seen anything like it."

"Is it really that unusual?"

"You didn't know?" she asked.

"Obviously," he said, "you've seen more naked men than I have."

"Well," she said. "I've never seen one that curves like this. Looks like it would fit inside me perfectly."

"Should we test out that theory?" he asked.

"Wait," she said, putting her hand against his chest. "You're not married, are you?"

"Not now, or ever, have I been married."

"Then definitely," she said. "Let's test it."

He mounted the hay bales with her. She lay down on her back and spread her legs. He pressed the head of his cock to her wet pussy, rubbed it there as if teasing her and then, when she was good and wet, he pushed hard enough to enter her.

Roxy sighed. "Oh yeah, that's good."

"It fits?" he asked.

She smiled. "It fits real good." In fact, she felt totally full, and as he started moving in her, she bit her lip. Not since Clint Adams had it felt this good to be with a man, to have a man inside of her . . . even Sam Starr, pretty man that he was, had pounded away at her. Dandy was moving slowly, gently, and she felt the pleasure building inside of her. He kept up that slow pace until she reached for him and said, "Okay, now harder."

And he gave her what she wanted . . .

Chapter Forty-Two

Later they were in the large bathtub, facing each other.

"Well," he said, "this wasn't exactly what I had in mind when I suggested we get to know each other better, but it'll do." He had one of her feet in his hands, and was massaging it. Her other foot was in the water, between his legs, her toes rubbing his penis and testicles.

"Oh yes," she said, "that will definitely do." She withdrew her foot from his hand "But we can't stay in here much longer. I don't look good when I'm all wrinkly."

She got out of the tub, grabbed his towel and began drying off.

"Well now, what am I supposed to do to get dry?" he asked.

"This is your place," she said, getting dressed. "Lock it up and walk around naked. The air will dry you."

"Right."

She grinned at him while she pulled on her boots and then, lastly, strapped on the gun, which had been within easy reach while she was in the tub.

"Where are you off to?" he asked.

"I'm supposed to meet Belle at the Onion," she said. "She's going to let me know who we're still waiting for."

"Including the man you're looking for?"

"What makes you think—"

"Come on," he said, "suddenly you were in no hurry to leave town. You must've heard that whoever you're looking for was on his way here."

"What a smart man you are."

"Roxy," he asked, "are you going to find more trouble than you can handle?"

"Jesus, I hope not." She went to the tub, leaned over and kissed him. "You're a nice man."

"What did you originally come over here for?" he asked.

"Oh," she said, "the horse, the gelding."

"He's in great shape," Dandy said. "I'm sure he'll take you wherever you want to go."

"That's good," she said. "Thank you."

"When will I see you again?" he asked.

"Jesus," she said, "I've been in and out of your place so much I thought you'd be sick of me by now."

"After this?" he said. "Not likely. Look, I have a house not far from here—"

"Dandy, I had a great time with you, but that's what it was."

"Nothing more, huh?"

"I'm sorry."

He sighed. "Then I guess I better dry off and get back to work."

"Whoa, whoa," she said, stopping him from standing up. "If I see that pretty curve again I may never get out of here. Just wait til I leave."

He settled back down in the tub and said, "If you do find out you need help, let me know."

"I'll do that," she said, opening the door, "especially if I get into trouble and need a vet."

***

She left the livery, her legs feeling light and rubbery, and headed for the Onion. When she got there she saw Belle sitting in as chair out front. There was another chair nearby, so she dragged it over and sat next to her.

Belle leaned over and smelled her.

"Oh, you dirty girl," she said, "Freshly bathed, I see, after goin' to see the vet."

"We got better acquainted," Roxy said, to reinforce her disinterest in Sam Starr.

"That's my girl!" Belle said. "I told you to find yourself a man and relax."

"And I did," Roxy said. "So what have you been up to?"

"I found Jellicoe and Wee Willie and made sure they know to keep their guns in their holsters."

"And Juarez?"

"He's still in a whorehouse, somewhere."

"And Sam?"

"Playin' poker."

"Nobody else is here yet?'

"If you mean Jesse," Belle said, "no."

"What about the men comin' with him?"

"If they're comin' with him," Belle said, "then they'll ride in with him. Why are you so interested in who he's bringin' along, anyway?"

Roxy shrugged.

"It's just good to know who you're going to be working with," she said. "Besides, you said you think Frank isn't in Missouri. Maybe he'll ride in, too."

"Well," Belle said, "that'd be good news."

"And maybe a Younger or two?" Roxy asked, referring to the Younger Brothers, who were famous for having ridden with Jesse and Frank James for a while.

"I doubt it," Belle said. "Not after the Northfield Raid. They lost two men in that one, and every one of them ended up getting' shot. That was the end."

"Weren't you married to a Younger for a while?" Roxy asked. "Cole's father?"

"That was a rumor," Belle said. "Never happened." She looked at Roxy. "You know how rumors spread."

"I do, indeed," Roxy said.

Belle looked out at the street. "It's just better to just let them lie."

"I agree."

"Lunch time," Belle said. "You hungry?"

"I worked up an appetite," Roxy said.

"Here comes Sam," Belle said, "and he looks hungry, too. Let's go inside and chow down."

Chapter Forty-Three

Sam Starr seemed less uncomfortable in Roxy's presence. She figured he now knew that she wasn't going to say anything to Belle about him sleeping with her. In fact, Roxy had no intention of ever telling anyone about that. It was a mistake she'd made, and didn't intend on repeating. No more married men. It was why she'd asked Dandy if he was married. If he'd said yes, she would have been out of there. She probably shouldn't have ever gone in once she saw that he was bathing, but there he was, naked as the day he was born, all pretty and clean. What else was she supposed to do?

Because Sam was relaxed they had more of a three way conversation than before, with him smiling and laughing. Maybe he'd won at poker, and it had put him in a good mood. But what Roxy was noticing was that the happier and friendlier Sam got, the more morose Belle became.

Finally, Belle seemed to have had it. "Enough of this shit!" she said, as the meal came to an end. "Sam, you better see that our horses are ready. Once Jesse gets here I want to be ready."

"Sure, Belle," he said, looking at her warily. "I'll take care of it."

"Roxy's already checked on her horse," Belle sad. "Our girl even got a better look at the vet, didn't you, Roxy?"

"Belle—"

"Aw, it's okay," Belle said, cutting her off. "Sam don't care if you had a romp and a poke with Dandy, do ya Sam?"

"Me?" Sam asked. "Why should I care?"

"Exactly!" Belle said. "Come on, let's get outta here."

***

Outside the hotel Belle once again pulled a chair over to sit while Sam made his way to the livery stable.

"Why did you say that about me and Dandy?" Roxy asked.

"Relax," Belle said, "now him and Sam will have something to talk about. Come on, sit."

Reluctantly, and for want of something better to do, Roxy sat.

"What's the problem?"

"I just don't like talking about my private affairs," Roxy groused.

"You think Sam's gonna think less of you?"

"I don't really care what Sam thinks of me, Belle," Roxy said. "You're obviously the leader of this gang."

"You're right about that," Belle said. "And everybody better understand that the way you do."

"Don't they?'

"I sometimes wonder—well, lookee here."

She cut herself off and pointed. Roxy looked out into the street and saw four riders coming. She recognized three of them, but not the fourth.

"Is that Jesse?" she asked.

"That, my dear girl," Belle Starr, "is Jesse James, himself."

Roxy felt elated.

The man she'd been searching for lately, Jed Harlow, was riding right alongside Jesse James. The other two men were the ones she had seen in Kingman with Harlow.

And she knew for sure Harlow and his cronies would recognize her.

Belle stood up, obviously so Jesse James would see her. Roxy's impression was that Belle had a world of respect for Jesse. The famed outlaw spotted her, and redirected his horse toward her. The others followed.

"Belle Starr!" Jesse called out. "You're lookin' as ornery as ever."

"Jesse James," Belle said. "You're lookin' older."

Jesse dismounted, came up on to the boardwalk and gave Belle a long hug, which she returned. The other three men watched the action without expression—until they saw Roxy.

"What the hell is she doin' here?" Jed Harlow asked.

Belle gave Harlow a hard look, then asked Jesse, "Who's your rude friend?"

"Belle, this is Jed Harlow, that's Ken Miller and Ollie Jenkins. Boys, this is Belle Starr, and you better treat her with respect. She's like a member of my family."

"I got no problem treating her with respect," Miller said, then pointed at Roxy, "but what's this bitch doin' here?"

"This bitch," Belle Starr said, "is a friend of mine and a member of this gang. If you're gonna be a member of the Starr gang, you better keep a civil tongue in your head."

Miller was about to respond but Jesse cut him off with a look.

"Get your horses taken care of," Belle said, "and then go inside and get your rooms. When you're all get cleaned up, we can talk."

"Is everybody here?" Jesse asked.

"Everybody was here but you," Belle said.

"Then we'll see you later," Jesse said.

Belle grabbed his arm as he turned to mount up, again.

"Talk to your people," she warned.

Jesse patted her hand and said, "Don't worry." He turned to Roxy and touched his hat. "A pleasure to meet you."

"Likewise," she said.

Jesse mounted up, and he, Harlow and the others headed for the livery.

"Okay," Belle said, "I don't like surprises. What's with you and those three."

"We had a run in down in Kingman, Arizona a while back," Roxy said. "Looks like they haven't got over it."

"And you have?"

Roxy shrugged. "There might be one or two things that still need clearing up."

"Can you clear them up quietly?"

"That might be up to them," Roxy said.

"Well," Belle said, "I need Jesse, I don't need them three. Lemme see if you can clear up your business without drivin' Jesse away."

"Done," Roxy said.

Chapter Forty-Four

Roxy made sure she wasn't sitting in front of the hotel when Jesse returned with Harlow and the other two. She was agreeable to letting Belle talk to Jesse before she confronted Harlow about his lies.

She had no idea how good or bad the lawman Sheriff Marks was. He seemed to be fine with the Belle Starr gang coming to Coffeyville, but then Belle had no intention of pulling a job right there in town, and seemed intent on keeping her men in line. And all that seemed to suit the lawman. But Roxy wanted to talk to him to figure out what her limitations were.

As she walked to the sheriff's office, she wondered how Belle Starr was going to react when she found out that Roxy was not going to be part of her gang, and had no intention of helping her pull her job, whatever it was. Five thousand or no five thousand. She knew that Lady Gunsmith might be looked upon as someone who straddled the fence when it came to which side of the law she was on, but up to this time in her life, she had never truly broken the law. She didn't intend to start now.

When she entered the office, the sheriff was seated at his desk, looking worried, and seeing her didn't improve his mood, any.

"Miss Doyle," he said. "Did Belle send you over here?"

"No, Sheriff," she said. "I'm here on my own."

"What can I do for you?"

"I want to get it clear in my head what kind of lawman you are," Roxy said.

"I do my job, Miss Doyle," he said.

"So Belle Starr and her gang are welcome here as long as they don't break the law."

"That's correct."

"And if I have a falling out with one of them, and push comes to shove, and somebody gets hurt . . . or worse . . ."

". . . I'll talk to witnesses, and act accordingly," Marks said. "Are you expecting trouble?"

"You know my reputation, Sheriff," Roxy said. "Even if I'm not looking for trouble, it seems to find me. Am I expecting it? Always."

"Well, I don't mind tellin' you," he said, "I'll be happy when you, Belle Starr and her gang ride out."

"Then you might be interested to know," she said, "that Jesse James just rode in."

Marks put his hands over his face and rubbed it.

"Well, Jesse did his time," he said. "He's welcome here, too, under the same conditions."

"Do you have deputies?" she asked.

"I'm supposed to have deputies," he said. "Two of 'em. But when Belle Starr comes to town, they find other things to be doin'."

"Ah."

"I don't suppose you'd—"

"No," she said, "wearing a star is not for me, Sheriff."

"Just thought I'd ask," he said. "Doesn't seem to me that being a part of the Starr gang is for you, either."

She almost told him she wasn't, but didn't want that statement getting back to Belle until she was ready to tell her, herself.

"Much obliged for your time, Sheriff."

Marks waved a hand and even before Roxy was out the door, went back to looking worried.

***

When Roxy went back to the Onion it was Sam Starr sitting out in front of the hotel, not Belle.

"Where's Belle?" she asked.

"Over at the Red Slipper with Jesse and the others."

Roxy looked in the direction of the Red Slipper, but didn't move.

"She said you had a beef with Jesse's friends."

"Are they his friends?" she asked. "Or are they just riding with him?"

"You'd have to ask Jesse."

"I don't want to mess things up for Belle with Jesse," Roxy said.

"Well, first of all Belle and Jesse consider themselves almost cousins," Sam said. "You ain't gonna mess anythin' up. Second, if you got a beef with one or all of those fellas let's get it out of the way right now. Better now than later."

"Good point."

Sam stood up. "You gonna need back up?"

"Nice of you to offer," Roxy said, "but I don't want to get you in trouble with Belle, either."

"I wasn't talkin' about me," Sam said.

"Who then?"

"Your vet friend."

"Dandy?"

Sam nodded. "Dandy ain't his real name. Ain't nobody around here but me and Belle know who he really is. And now Jesse, when he sees him."

"I don't understand."

"If you and him have got as close as I think you have," Sam said, "he'll back any play you make."

"With a gun?" Roxy asked. "You mean he's not really a vet?"

"He knows how to treat most animal's ailments," Sam said. "Most of us do, who've lived around them. He's only been the vet here less than a year, and luckily he ain't had any real bad cases to treat. He's just sorta hangin' his hat here until he decides what he really wants."

"So he's living here under an assumed name?"

"That's right."

"Dandy . . . what?"

"Just Dandy."

"And Jesse knows him?"

Sam nodded. "Real well."

"Then why wouldn't Dandy leave knowing Jesse's on his way?" she asked.

Sam shrugged. "Guess he feels it's time for him to come outta hidin'. Well, not hidin' really, more like . . ."

215

"Exile?"

"That's it!" Sam said. "But the kind you do to yourself."

"Self-imposed?"

"You're a smart girl."

"Why are you telling me this?"

"Because I never thought you was here to join the Starr gang," Sam said. "It's not your style. Belle can't see that, but I can. So you're here for another reason—and I think it just rode into town, today."

"It's Harlow, and his two friends," Roxy confessed. "He lied to me, sent me on a wild goose chase to Ellsworth, Kansas, tellin' me my Pa died there."

"Your Pa?"

"Gavin Doyle."

"The bounty hunter?"

"That's right."

"Ain't he dead?" Sam saw the look on her face and backed off immediately. "I mean, I ain't heard nothin' about him in a while."

"Well, Harlow said he was killed in Ellsworth, it was an out-and-out lie. I *knew* it and still went there. Stupid move."

"Well," Sam said, "don't make another one, Roxy. If you're gonna face Harlow you'll have to go against the other two, as well."

"And Jesse?"

"I don't know," Sam said. "That's somethin' you're gonna have to find out the hard way, mebbe."

"What about Belle?"

"She'll stay out of it, as long as it's between you and Harlow. But don't try to make her pick between you and Jesse. That's one you'll lose. I ain't even sure she'd pick me over Jesse. To her he's family, and those roots go back."

"Thanks for this, Sam," she said. "Maybe I'll go and talk to Dandy—or whatever his real name is."

"It's Frank James," Sam said. "He's Jesse's brother.

Chapter Forty-Five

First, Roxy couldn't believe that Dandy was Frank James, and that she had slept with him.

Second, she didn't believe that Jesse didn't know his own brother was in Coffeyville, living as the town vet.

And third, she didn't want to involve Frank, but if there was a chance it would put him at odds with his brother.

Sam left her in front of the hotel to go meet Belle at the Red Slipper. She sat there, considering her options, and decided not to go to the livery to talk with Frank—Dandy. Suddenly, she remembered something the fortune teller, Madame Helga, had told her in Ellsworth.

"There is a man who is not who he says he is."

Was she talking about Frank James, warning her? Even if it wasn't a warning, just a piece of information, it was eerily true.

And she told her there were men who would try to kill her. Like the one who had taken shots at her the night before? Or maybe Harlow and his two friends?

She took out her gun, checked the action, made sure it was fully loaded, and then slid it back into her holster. Sam Starr was right about one thing. It would be better to get this over with as soon as possible.

She stood up, adjusted her gunbelt, then started over to the Red Slipper.

***

When she entered the Slipper it was even more crowded than the night before. She could hear chips hitting the table, and a roulette wheel going around. She stopped just inside the doorway and let her eyes flow over the scene. She finally spotted Belle and Sam Starr sitting at a table with Jesse James. That meant that the others were elsewhere. She had no idea if, when she faced Jed Harlow, Belle's other men—Jellicoe, Wee Willie and Alfredo Juarez—would stand with him. If they did, and it came to gunplay, she was in trouble.

Then she saw Belle's men at another table. Still no sign of Harlow and his, but this was a good omen, she thought, that they weren't sitting with Belle, Sam and Jesse.

And then she heard Harlow's loud bark of a laugh. It came from the bar, and she saw him standing there with Miller and the other man. Harlow had his arm around a saloon girl, who was trying to get away from him. That was why he was laughing.

"You're stayin' right here, gal," he said, loudly.

"Let me go," the girl said, struggling. "I have work to do."

"Yeah, you do," Harlow said. "You're gonna make me and my friends happy men."

"Let her go!" Roxy shouted.

Harlow heard, as did some of the other men at the bar. Heads turned and took her in. Some men smiled, others frowned.

"What did you say?" Harlow asked.

"I said 'let the girl go,'" Roxy said. "You and me got business. You can play with her later."

Harlow stared at Roxy, then dropped his arm from the girl's waist. She was shocked, and stood there for a moment.

"Move, girl!" Roxy snapped.

The saloon girl ran.

"It's that bitch from Kingman, Jed," Miller said.

"I see 'er," Harlow said. "Whataya mean, we got business?"

"You sent me on a fool's errand to Ellsworth," Roxy said. "You lied, like I knew you were, but I went, anyway."

"That'd make you a fool, all right," Harlow said, and barked out his laugh.

"Well, this fool is here to make you pay," Roxy said. "I want the truth, or else . . ."

"Or else what, girl?" Harlow sneered

"You'll find out."

Miller moved to one side of Harlow, and Jenkins moved to the other. All three stood with their backs to the bar, facing Roxy. Roxy moved a few feet to her left for a better angle, and men cleared out from their tables and moved away.

It got deadly quiet . . .

***

Jesse made a move, as if to get up from the table, but Belle put her hand on his arm to stop him.

"Ain't she with you?" he asked.

"Yeah," Belle said, "and they're with you."

"But three against one . . ." he said.

She patted his arm. "This might be interestin'."

"She might get killed."

"Yeah," Belle said, "she might . . ."

***

Roxy knew that when facing this many men, she had to identify the one in charge. That was Harlow. The other two wouldn't draw until he did, so she kept her eyes right on him. And she knew that, hell or high water, whatever happened to her, she was at least going to kill him.

Then a man stepped through the batwings.

"Just hold it!" he snapped.

Roxy saw Dandy—or Frank James—standing there with a gun strapped on.

"Mind yer business, friend," Harlow said. "This is between girlie and me."

"This lady happens to be a friend of mine," Frank James said. "That makes it my business."

"Fair enough," Harlow said. "I'll just kill ya both."

"Frank?" a voice called out. "Is that you?"

Frank James didn't take his eyes off of Harlow, but he said, "It's me, Jesse. How ya been, brother?"

"Good," Jesse said, stepping from a group of men. "What're ya doin' here?"

"Just layin' low til I decide what I wanna do with my life," Frank said.

"Didn't know you wuz this close to home," Jesse said.

"That was kinda the point, Jess."

"Wait a minute," Harlow said, confused. "You're Frank James?"

"That's right."

"And if this gal is a friend of my brother's," Jesse said, moving across the room to stand next to Frank, "then she's a friend of mine, too."

"Hold on," Harlow said. "We ride with you, Jesse."

"You did, Harlow," Jesse said. "Now you don't."

"I think," Frank said, "you're right—Harlow, is it?"

"Yep."

"This is between you and the girl," Frank said. "You other two stand aside, or deal with us."

"Jesse?" Harlow said.

"That's how it is, Jed," Jesse said. "Frank's my brother. I stand with him. Miller, you and Jenkins stand aside."

Miller didn't like it, but Roxy could see he wasn't about to go up against the James boys. He moved, and Jenkins moved with him.

That left her and Jed Harlow.

"Now first," Roxy said, "you're going apologize for sending me to Ellsworth."

"You're crazy!"

"Then you're going to tell me what you know about my Pa."

"Your Pa?" Harlow said. "Oh, you mean Gavin Doyle."

"That's right."

"Well, he was a no good coward," Harlow said, "and he died that way, beggin' for mercy."

"Now again," Roxy said, "I know you're lying, and this time I ain't going to stand for it."

"Bitch," Harlow said, "you ain't gettin' an apology. Yer gettin' a bullet."

Harlow went for his gun.

Over the past five years it had started to happen for Roxy the way Clint Adams told her it happened for him. She was so fast that the men she opposed looked as if they were moving in slow motion. She saw Harlow's hand go for the gun in his holster and she outdrew him so cleanly his weapon never cleared leather.

Nobody in the room saw her gun hand move, and she shot him dead center in the chest.

Harlow was thrown back against the bar by the force of the bullet, then slumped to the floor, dead.

"Jesus," somebody said. Roxy thought it was Jesse, which pleased her.

She holstered her gun, turned to Miller and Jenkins.

"Well, now he's dead and he can't tell me the truth," she said, "so start talking, Miller."

"M-me? Why m-me?" Miller asked.

"Because I don't like you," she said. "Not one bit. So you're going to tell me what Harlow knew about my Pa."

"H-he didn't know nothin'," Miller said. "He was a big talker."

"Somebody in Hays heard him say he knew what happened to my father."

"Hays, was it?" Miller asked. "H-he was tellin' lies in Hays. Whoppers, he was tellin'."

"Is that right?" Roxy asked Jenkins.

"That's right, Ma'am," Jenkins said. "Harlow was a big blowhard. I ain't mad you killed 'im, no, sir, not at all."

"Me, neither!" Miller chimed in. "No, sir!"

They both put their hands in the air, away from their guns.

"We ain't got nothin' against you, Ma'am," Jenkins said.

"And nothin' against you boys," Miller said to Jesse and Frank.

"What do you wanna do, Roxy?' Frank asked.

She took her gun out, causing Miller and Jenkins to flinch, ejected the empty shell, reloaded it and slid it back.

"Let them go," she said.

"Get out of town, boys," Frank said. "Now!"

"Y-yessir," Miller said. "We're gettin'."

"And take that with you," Jesse said, pointing to Harlow.

"Yessir!" Jenkins said.

They each grabbed a leg and dragged Harlow toward the door. hey passed Roxy along the way, and Miller stopped and looked at her.

"I don't know if this means nothin'," he said, "but Harlow mentioned somethin' about your old man and Denver. Somethin' about a job. You might wanna go there and check."

"Thanks," she said. At least that gave her a direction in which to go.

They dragged Harlow out to the street.

"What the hell—" Sheriff Marks said, stepping aside to let them out, and then coming inside. "What the hell happened?"

"I can explain, Sheriff," Roxy said.

Marks looked at her. "Please do."

Epilogue

Roxy didn't get to talk to anyone—Belle, Sam, Jesse or Frank—until the next morning. She went to the sheriff's office with Marks straight from the saloon and told him the whole story. Then she went to the Onion. She was mad. She'd wasted months of her time on Jed Harlow, who turned out to be nothing but a liar, like most men. So she wanted nothing to do with anybody the rest of the night, and remained in her room.

She woke feeling lost. What was her next move? Should she ride with Belle Starr and Jesse James? Or just ride aimlessly, until she heard something else about her Pa?

Whatever she decided, she was getting out of town today. She went down to the front desk to check out, then carried her saddlebags and rifle to the livery.

"Dandy!" she called, then corrected herself. "Frank?"

"Back here!" he called.

She went to the back room where she had seen him bathing. The bathtub was empty, and he was packing things into a pair of saddlebags.

"What are you up to?" she asked.

"Packing to leave," he said. "I'm goin' back to Missouri with Jesse."

"Would you be doing that if you hadn't helped me?"

He turned to look at her. "Jesse'd still be here, so yeah, I guess I would."

"Well, I want to thank you for helping me last night. Thank Jesse too, for me."

"I will." He turned to face her. "Where are you off to, Roxy?"

"I don't know," she said. "I'm still trying to decide. Probably Denver, although I can't really trust what Miller was saying. Still, it's something."

"Well, take my advice and don't go with Belle."

"Why not?"

"You ain't the type to ride with the likes of her."

"I thought you and Jesse liked her."

"Hell, we love 'er," Frank said. "But she ain't for you, Roxy. And actually, this job of hers ain't for Jesse. He listened to her offer, and turned her down."

"Why?"

"She was gonna start targeting Missouri banks," Frank said. "Jesse and me, we want no part of that. We hope you won't, either."

"I guess I'll tell her that, then," she said. "I'm going to saddle my horse and ride out. See you again some time, Frank."

"Maybe, Roxy," Frank said. "Maybe." He went back to packing. She was wondering why he was being so stand offish, not even offering her a hug. Well, if that was the way he wanted it.

She went and saddled the new gelding.

**

As she rode past the Onion, Belle came out with Sam. They saw her and waited for her to reach them.

"You headin' out, too?" Belle asked.

"Sorry, Belle," she said. "Robbin' banks ain't for me."

"Not for Jesse or Frank, either," she said. "Least ways, Missouri banks."

"You going ahead with it?" Roxy asked.

"Naw," Belle said. "Lost us too many men here, plus you. Guess we'll head on back to the territories. Heard Deputy Bas Reeves is lookin for us. Might be interestin'."

"Well, so long" Roxy said.

"So long, Roxy," Sam said.

Belle looked at Sam, then back at Roxy.

"I got some advice for you, girl," she said.

"What's that?"

"Stay away from married men,"

So, she knew. Or did Sam tell her?

"Belle," Roxy said, "honest, I didn't know!"

"Didn't know what?" Belle asked.

"Well . . . what are you talking about?"

"I'm talking about Frank," Belle said. "He's got a wife back in Missouri."

Jesus, Roxy thought, they all lie.

"What did you think I was talking about?" Belle asked.

"Frank," Roxy said, "I just thought you were talking about Frank."

She waved at them and as she rode up the street she heard Belle say to Sam, "What the hell did she think I was talkin' about, Sam?"

Coming May 2017

Lady Gunsmith 2
The Three Graves of Roxy Doyle

By
AWARD-WINNING AUTHOR
J.R. Roberts

For more information
visit: www.speakingvolumes.us

ANGEL EYES *series*
by
Award-Winning Author
Robert J. Randisi (J.R. Roberts)

Visit us at www.speakingvolumes.us

TRACKER *series*
by
Award-Winning Author
Robert J. Randisi (J.R. Roberts)

Visit us at www.speakingvolumes.us

MOUNTAIN JACK PIKE *series*
by
Award-Winning Author
Robert J. Randisi (J.R. Roberts)

Visit us at www.speakingvolumes.us